Woody Lake Mysteries

MALICE Aforecourt

BETWIXT and Bewitched

A Christmas in July SUNDOWNER SALLY

DEATH by Candlelight
GRAVE Double

GRAVE Double

A Woody Lake Mystery
Book #4

Rennae Todd

Jakada Books
PERTH, WESTERN AUSTRALIA

Grave Double: format (novel) / Rennae Todd / Jakada Books / Perth Western Australia

Publisher's Note: This is a work of fiction. Names, characters, places, and incidents are a product of the author's imagination. Locales and public names are sometimes used for atmospheric purposes. Any resemblance to actual people, living or dead, or to businesses, companies, events, institutions, or locales is completely coincidental.

D2D edition ISBN: 978-0-6459953-9-8

In this Story

Grave Double is the fourth and final title in the Woody Lake Mystery series set in the fictional outer-Perth suburbs of Woody Lake and Rosny, located on either side of the Cygnet River.

In this story, Hettie, Marlee and the Mrs. B's visit the old cemetery and discover a burial that shouldn't be there. While definitely not investigating a murder, Hettie gets involved with investigating a family history that her friend and fellow croquet player, Belle Danvers, has been asked to ghostwrite. What possible complications could that cause, even if the family history does involve the body they found?

And will her new croquet courts go some way to mending Hettie's fraught relationship with her mother or will the death she's not investigating be the end of her plans.

Main Characters

<u>Parke Family</u>

Henrietta (Hettie) Parke: (48) Relief teacher, president of the Parke Croquet. Divorced from Brian Hitchcock (deceased). Lives at 6 Old Dairy Road.

Ceefer: a black cat recently arrived in Hettie's life. Has talents not yet fully understood.

Violet Hitchcock: Hettie's daughter (22). Runs the Club Cafe. Lives with Hettie.

Elly and Rafe Figeroa: Hettie's daughter (27), works part-time in advertising, Rafe is a landscape designer, daughters Jazmin (4) and Rosa (2). Live at 4 Old Dairy Road.

Jack and California (Callie) Parke: Hettie's parents. Live in a villa unit at Sunny Vale Retirement Village.

Alice Slater: Alice is Jack's Parke's younger sister, widowed. Lives at 8 Old Dairy Road.

Larry and Gwen Parke: Hettie's brother (46). Plays bowls. They run Parke Real Estate Agency. Live at 2 Old Dairy Road.

Pearl, Max and Maxxie Longchamp: Hettie's younger sister (37). Married to businessman Max. Son Maxxie (20) is a university student. Lived at 10 Old Dairy Road, now live on Rosny Circle.

Eddie, Gloria and Frank Garcia: Related to Callie Parke. Eddie is a retired plumber. Son Frank is a primary school sports teacher. Eddie's sister Gloria favours conspiracy theories. They occupy two houses further along Old Dairy Road.

Croquet Club Members

Judy Sanford: nurse, Hettie's friend.

Romola Asquith: Club Secretary, Hettie's friend.

Belle Danvers: ghostwriter, Hettie's friend .

Andrew Asquith: accountant, Club treasurer, Romola's brother-in-law.

Bowls Club Members

George Engles: President.

Gary Asquith: Romola's husband.

Sandra Alberts: Committee member, dog Brutus.

Others

Detective Inspector Grayson Fox: Homicide squad. Someone Hettie once.

Sergeant Stuart Higgins: In charge of Rosny Police Station.

Dan Wallace: reporter for the *Rosny Record.*

Mrs. Edith Braxton and Mrs. Ila Bronson: known as the Mrs. B's. They frequent the Club Cafe and live nearby on Old Dairy Road.

Janelle Rice: knew Ceefer's previous owner, Miranda. Has a white Persian named Aurora who is Ceefer's troublesome friend.

Marlee Grainger: Hettie's friend and former teacher, now a librarian at the Battye Library of West Australian history

Parke Trust

Bladen (Den) Barrett: former mayor of Cygnet LGA.

Isolde Reflex: lawyer.

Darla Dalrymple: owner of Top Cut Hair Salons.

Chapter 1

Hettie locked the door to the croquet patio behind the last club member and stared out at the three new courts under development behind her existing three. She still found it hard to believe it was really happening. It had seemed sometimes during the past year that her new courts would remain a pipe dream. Unfortunately, there were some in the community who thought that was just where they should have stayed.

"We're losing our public park to a private club," one letter to the Editor of the *Rosny Record* claimed. "Ordinary people losing out to the sporting elite. They need to be called to account." And "How much is this costing us?" cried another.

It upset Callie. Just as Hettie felt she and her mother were making headway towards a more amiable relationship, this assault on the Parke name set her off again.

"First it's murder, and now it's your club," she complained to Hettie. Which was rich,

Hettie felt, considering her mother had been encouraging her to raise the Croquet Club's profile and associate something positive with the family name after three murders.

Eventually, and no doubt at Callie's insistence, the Parke Trust had issued a statement in the *Rosny Record* explaining that no public money was spent on maintaining the park and lake, and that the land was, in fact, made available to the public through the philanthropy of the late Terrence Parke and his family. As for the Clubs, they were self-supporting and available to anyone to join on payment of the requisite membership fee.

The Trust's statement didn't completely stop the grumbles. The complaints then shifted to 'giving with one hand and taking with the other.' Hettie wondered if some people simply enjoyed having something to complain about.

The new courts weren't ready for use yet, but the grass had been laid and top dressed, and there was a temporary fence separating them from the original courts. In six weeks, her dream of holding some of the National Tournament events at the Parke Croquet Club in Woody Lake would become a reality.

She forced herself to turn away from the view. Friends and fellow club members Judy Sanford, Romola Asquith and Belle Danvers were already in the Cafe, and she was supposed to be joining them for lunch. It was Belle's birthday. Despite the cakes for morning tea, Belle wasn't ready to end her celebrations just yet. Hettie decided a salad would be a wise choice for lunch. She headed toward the back of the croquet room and the private entrance to the Cafe.

"Hettie." George Engles' voice halted her, and she turned back reluctantly. The Bowls Club president was approaching from the passage that accessed their offices, kitchen, and bathrooms, and the Bowls Club's room. His normally pleasant, square face was twisted into a scowl.

"What is it, George?" Hettie asked trying to appear upbeat. "I'm late for lunch."

"Someone's been throwing rubbish onto our greens again. Apple cores, rotten bananas, squashed peaches."

"Well, that's a waste of good fruit," Hettie said lightly.

George's voice rose a notch. "It's not a joking matter. This is the second time this week. It's all the attention in the papers about your courts taking away some of the park area that's causing it. It's upsetting people."

Hettie wished Larry were here right now. Her brother was always able to calm George, but he was away down south with Gwen for a long weekend break. She'd always got on well with George herself, once upon a time, before he became president and started getting upset about her plans for expansion.

"I'm sorry, George," Hettie responded, determined not to escalate the matter. "If it happens again you might want to report it to Sergeant Higgins. Have you thought of putting CCTV cameras outside?"

"Well, if I did, the Croquet Club should be paying for them. This is all your fault."

Hettie stared at him for a moment. "We haven't had a problem with rubbish, George. Funny it's the bowling greens that are being targeted and not the croquet courts. You sure you haven't upset someone?"

"I should never have agreed to any of this," George muttered, and stomped off back the way he'd come. Hettie shook her head and went into the Cafe.

"Merrow," Ceefer greeted her as she entered the main room. He was sitting by the Mrs. B's table as usual. They did spoil him.

"Hello, to you, too," she said, stopping to rub behind his ears.

4

"How are you, Hettie?" the elderly Mrs. Braxton asked. "Your new courts are looking very nice."

"I'm fine, thank you. Yes, they are, aren't they?"

"You must be excited. Not long now. I remember when you first asked for more land. Some people weren't happy about losing a bit of the park, you know, but I always said…"

"We know all that, Edith, it's history," Mrs. Bronson broke in. "Don't hold Hettie up, now. Her friends are waiting to order."

"I was just saying…"

"You're always just saying, Edith," Mrs. Bronson interrupted again.

Hettie left them to it. She had come to the conclusion years ago that the two elderly friends enjoyed their little squabbles, but Mrs. Bronson had sounded more acerbic than usual. She joined the girls in the booth along the side wall, overlooking the shade garden.

"We were about to send out a search party for you," Belle said as Hettie slid in beside Judy.

""I was waylaid by George," Hettie explained.," Hettie explained. "Someone's been throwing rubbish on the bowling greens, and it's all our fault for the newspaper attention we've been getting. I suggested CCTV cameras and he said the Croquet Club should pay for them."

"That's a bit over the top," Belle said.

Tess, her hair today a vibrant pink, came over to take their order as Violet attended to a customer at the counter. With orders placed, and coffee and water in front of them, they forgot about George and his rubbish for the moment.

"So, what's this project you have to work on today," Romola asked Belle.

"It's a family history job," Belle replied, brushing back her long, curly red hair. "The woman is researching her grandmother's story, but she's a horticulturalist, and needs help putting the words together." Which was what ghostwriter Belle made her living at, of course.

"But why today?" Romola persisted. "Surely you could have put her off on your birthday."

"I couldn't. She's only here for the weekend. She's staying at an Airbnb in Rosny but leaving for home again tomorrow afternoon," Belle explained.

"Who is she researching?" Hettie asked. "There must be a connection here if she's visiting."

"She could be here just to see Belle," Judy reasoned.

"Of course, she could."

"That's it, I imagine," Belle replied. "She found my website and decided she needed some help. She's from Denmark."

"Oh."

Belle laughed. "Not Denmark in Scandinavia. Denmark, Western Australia."

That wasn't what had surprised Hettie. It was because Denmark was where Gwen and Larry were spending part of their four-day break. "I'll let you know if my client has dug up any juicy stories about your families," Belle added with a wink.

"Hardly likely," Judy replied. "None of us have been here as far back as our grandmothers."

"Except for Hettie," Romola reminded her.

"I've heard enough about my family history recently, thank you very much," Hettie said.

"Well, I'm sure you'll make it an interesting read, Belle, whatever the grandmother's story," Judy told her, as their food arrived.

As they ate, Hettie thought again of George Engles and his claim that her new croquet courts were causing problems for the Bowls Club. It was unpleasant to have disagreements between the clubs when they occupied the same building.

"What do you think about us holding an Open Day to celebrate the new courts?" she asked her friends. "If we involve the Bowls Club it might make George feel better about what we're doing, and show people we're not this private, exclusive club some believe us to be."

"You want to do this before the Nationals of course." Romola, as Club Secretary, kept an eye on timetables.

"Say in four weeks?" Hettie said.

"That's not a bad idea," Judy agreed, as Romola and Belle both nodded. "If we can get it up in time. What sort of things would we do?"

"We could have some of our players taking visitors around the court for a game with a bit of coaching," Romola said.

"Balloons, food trucks, a magician," Belle put in.

"A magician?"

"To keep the kids amused while their parents try out croquet."

"That's a good idea. I'll talk to Vi about what the Cafe can do, and what food trucks we might want," Hettie said.

"We have a committee meeting next week," Romola reminded them. "Doesn't give us much time."

"I'll set up as much as possible beforehand," Hettie promised. "Dan could give us some advertising, too." Having a reporter as a potential future son-in-law was proving more useful than Hettie would have imagined. "And I'll talk to George about the Bowls Club holding some attractions at the same time. If he thinks they might get some new members it could cheer him up."

With plans for the event put in motion, conversation for the remainder of lunch focused on Western Australia's chances of winning the Interstate Shield at the Nationals, and whether their state's top player could take out another gold medal.

As they were leaving to go their separate ways after lunch, Hettie's phone rang. She waved her friends off as she answered it, standing in the Cafe garden.

"Marlee how are you?" she greeted the caller.

"Hettie, are you busy this afternoon?" Marlee, never one to waste words, wanted to know.

"Ah, no, not unless you count housework. Why, what's up?"

"I want to visit that cemetery of yours for my project. Can you come with me? You can give me some background while we're there."

"Um, yeah, sure. What time?"

"I can be at yours at two."

"You've got my address?"

"I do. And my GPS. Thanks, Hettie. I appreciate it."

"It'll by good to see you." They ended the call.

"Well, that's more fun than vacuuming the house, anyway."

"What is?" asked a voice behind her.

Hettie spun around, realising she'd spoken aloud. Mrs. Bronson was looking at her quizzically.

"I thought it was only old people who talked to themselves," Mrs. Braxton commented.

"Well, you would know," Mrs. Bronson said.

Hettie frowned. What was going on with these two? The sharp edge to Mrs. Bronson's comments didn't seem to have improved over lunch.

"I've been invited to accompany a friend to visit the old cemetery this afternoon," Hettie replied.

"Whatever for?" Mrs. Bronson snapped. So, it wasn't just Mrs. Braxton she was being sharp with.

"Marlee's a librarian at the Battye Library and she's documenting the old cemeteries in the state."

"We haven't been able to go there this year, have we Ila?" Mrs. Braxton said.

Hettie knew they put flowers on her grandmother's grave each year around the anniversary of Florrie Parke's death. The three of them had been close friends.

"And I suppose that's my fault," Mrs. Bronson snapped back.

"Oh, Ila, for goodness' sake. We can't help getting older. It comes from living." Mrs. Braxton replied, losing patience.

"Hmph." Ila Bronson moved off past them without another word, which was when Hettie noticed she was moving carefully and using a walking stick. She and Mrs. Braxton watched as Mrs. Bronson made her way slowly through the Cafe garden, heading for her home across Old Dairy Road.

"She's unwell?" Hettie asked.

"It's her hip," Mrs. Braxton explained, a note of sadness and concern in her voice. "The doctor's talking about an operation and a replacement. She's not taken it well, poor love."

"I'm sorry to hear that," Hettie said. "About the operation, I mean. I imagine she wouldn't be able to get up the hill to the cemetery right now."

"No, she couldn't. That's the problem."

"But you could, couldn't you? Why don't you come with Marlee and me today?" Hettie offered on the spur of the moment.

"I really don't want to go without Ila," Mrs. Braxton said regretfully. It was clear to Hettie she was torn about refusing. "I did think of going by myself, but I don't like being out there alone. It is quite isolated."

"It is," Hettie agreed, imagining how an elderly lady would feel by herself, with nothing but open paddocks dotted with a few straggly eucalypts, and a cemetery on a hill. She thought quickly.

"What if Mrs. Bronson comes with us but waits in the car? And I video you putting the flowers on Grandma's grave?"

"With Ila's phone?" Mrs. Braxton said eagerly. "Oh, would you Hettie? It would cheer her up no end."

"I don't know how long Marlee is planning on being there, though. You might have to wait in the car for some time."

"That's fine. I'll go back to the car after I've laid the flowers, and we'll watch the video together. It will be lovely." She pulled Hettie into a hug. "Thank you so much, Hettie. You're as lovely as Florrie. She'd be so proud of you."

Hettie felt tears well up as she returned Edith Braxton's hug. Her grandmother had been a lovely person. A little absent-minded at times, but sweet and caring with it. And she'd had a lot to deal with, having a daughter-in-law like Callie.

"How long have we got?" Mrs. Braxton asked. Hettie told her. "I need to go tell Ila and order the flowers." She squeezed Hettie's arm before rushing off across the Road to Ila Bronson's house, next door to her own.

Chapter 2

"I hope you don't mind," Hettie said to
Marlee, as her friend drove her Pajero down
Old Dairy Road to collect the Mrs. B's.

"Not at all. Only too glad to help," Marlee
assured her. The florist's van was just
disappearing up the road as they pulled up.
Their passengers were waiting, sitting out front
of Mrs. Bronson's house with a basket, and a
bouquet of flowers.

They both got to their feet. Mrs. Braxton
folded the chairs and carried them to the
vehicle.

"Just as well you have a nice big car," she
said, as both Marlee and Hettie hopped out to
help.

Hettie introduced the Mrs. B's to her friend,
and she and Marlee proceeded to pack the
ladies, their chairs, and the basket, full of
afternoon tea, into the car. Packing in Mrs.
Bronson required extra care and an upturned
plant pot as a step. The front passenger seat
was moved as far forward as it would go to

allow room as she settled in. Fortunately, she wasn't a large lady,

"Thank you for thinking of us, Hettie," Mrs. Bronson said, as they made their way out of Woody Lake and onto the back road that led past the cemetery.

"You're most welcome," Hettie assured her, glad to see she was sounding more chipper than she'd been earlier. The drive only took ten minutes, and when they arrived, they discovered they were not alone. Another vehicle was parked by the side of the road below the cemetery, a red Nissan X-Trail.

"I wonder who that can be," Hettie said. She didn't recognise it.

"Do you get many visitors to the cemetery?" Marlee asked. "Presuming that's why they're here."

"I wouldn't have thought so."

"Don't forget to take the video," Mrs. Bronson said, handing her phone to Mrs. Braxton.

"Are you going to sit out, Ila," Mrs. Braxton asked, as she, Hettie, and Marlee got out of the car.

"Not just yet," Mrs. Bronson said, eying the other vehicle. "Would you mind locking the doors? I'll just have this window down a little."

Marlee obliged. Hettie could understand Mrs. Bronson's concern.

"I wonder if it's stolen and been dumped here," she said. There was a thin layer of dust on the Nissan, as if it had been standing there a day or two. She looked around. There was no one in sight, although they wouldn't be able to see anyone if they were among the trees at the cemetery.

"Well, lead the way," Marlee said to Hettie. "We'll soon find out if anyone else is here."

Hettie opened the gate, and they started up the dry tussocky slope of the paddock to the little cemetery nestled among the scraggy mallee eucalypts at the top. The collection of unmarked grave mounds, headstones, and the odd scrap of wood, that must at some time been part of a cross marking a grave, looked much the same as it had when Hettie had been here last. Except for the crows.

Several of the birds, cawing mournfully, flew up into the trees at their approach. Hettie shivered. She could well understand why Mrs. Braxton didn't want to come here alone. She didn't recall it being this dreary when Uncle Roscoe was interred less than a year ago. A cloud passed over the sun adding to the gloomy atmosphere.

"It feels as if spirits are walking about here," Marlee said, pulling out her phone and beginning to photograph the various graves.

"I'll just put the flowers on Florrie's grave and get back to Ila," Mrs. Braxton said. Hettie thought Mrs. Braxton was feeling spooked as well. And there was no one here belonging to the Nissan either.

"We need to make the video worthwhile," Hettie told her, opening the camera app on Mrs. Bronson's phone. "I'll do a little sweep and then follow you walking over to Grandma's grave." Marlee stepped back out of range as Hettie panned the camera slowly across the cemetery before bringing the focus back to Mrs. Braxton with her flowers. "All right now, off you go."

Mrs. Braxton walked across to the two graves on the far side. Surrounded by a low decorative iron railing, they had a single shared headstone. Bending down she placed the bouquet of white chrysanthemums and multicoloured zinnias at the head of the grave closest to her. A crow cawed from the trees above and she jumped, turning quickly away. Hettie stopped the video.

"Here you are," she said, handing her the phone. She hoped Mrs. Bronson wouldn't be disappointed.

"Thank you, Hettie. I'll see you back at the car." Mrs. Braxton scurried off down the slope.

Marlee continued to take photos. "When was the last burial here?" she asked.

Hettie told her about Uncle Roscoe, and before that Aunt Alice's first husband, Alan Miller, and both her grandparents, Terry and Florrie Parke.

"Are all you Parke's going to be buried here? I didn't think that was allowed."

"Only up to and including my father's generation if they choose to. It was worked out in the development proposal."

"Sounds like strings pulled, if you ask me," Marlee commented. Hettie had a distinct feeling Marlee didn't agree with that method. Hettie hadn't been born when Woody Lake was established, so had no say in the development proposal.

Marlee took some close-up shots of the headstones, one of which was lying sideways, and of the scrappy remains of several wooden crosses.

"Well, I think we might leave it at that," Marlee said, taking one last photo. "It isn't the most cheerful spot, is it?"

"Not today, certainly."

They started back down the slope. The Nissan still sat unattended, and the Mrs. B's were both in Marlee's vehicle. As they got closer, Mrs. Braxton got out, leaving the car door open, and started back up toward them, waving, and stumbling a little in her haste.

Hettie started to run to meet her, wondering what had upset the woman, because it was clear she was upset about something. Then she saw Mrs. Braxton was waving a phone. Had she received a distressing call?

"There's someone there," Mrs. Braxton panted, her eyes big in a face now pale as she thrust the phone at Hettie. "Someone's buried there."

"Well, yes, but…"

"Look, look at the video. Ila saw it first, and then she enlarged it. Look, here right in the corner of the picture, on Roscoe's grave."

Hettie watched as Mrs. Braxton enlarged the video image with a shaky finger, panning across it a little.

"Here, see."

Hettie took the phone. "What is that?"

Something was poking up out of the dirt on Uncle Roscoe Slater's grave.

"It's fingers," Mrs. Braxton all but whispered. "That's what it is, isn't it? Doesn't it look like fingers? And those crows…"

Hettie felt a little sick. It did look like fingers. Almost skeletal fingers. And there was that empty car down on the road.

"Let me see." Marlee took the phone from Hettie.

"Could just be a twig," she said, peering at it. "Could be just the angle making it look a bit - spooky."

Hettie sighed. "We need to check it out, though," she said, turning back and starting up the slope once more. "Anyone else coming?"

"I am," Mrs. Braxton said, following. Marlee didn't move. They heard a car door slam and looked back. Mrs. Bronson, it seemed, had locked herself in again. Marlee must have decided she didn't want to be left alone standing halfway down the hill and started up after them.

Reaching the cemetery was like a replay of their first arrival. The crows cawed and flew up into the trees again, only this time Hettie saw where they'd flown from. She approached Uncle Roscoe's grave, moving around to the foot for a different perspective than what the video had shown them.

Marlee and Mrs. Braxton stood and watched, not saying anything. What Hettie saw looked like three fingers exposed down to the second knuckle, stripped bare of flesh. The crows had been scratching away at the soil, and the soil seemed loose, too loose for a grave filled in twelve months ago. It didn't have the compaction from time and weather that she would have expected.

She picked up a stick and scraped a little around the fingers until the tip of the pinkie finger came into view.

"There's a ring," Hettie said quietly, dropping the stick she was using and straightening up. "I can't do any more. I might disturb some evidence. I think it's a woman. She must be buried with her head to the foot of the grave."

"Oh, my goodness," Mrs. Braxton gasped, her hand going to her mouth.

Marlee just shook her head as if in disbelief. Hettie pulled her phone from her pants pocket and tapped on her contacts. Sergeant Stuart Higgins answered on the second ring.

"Stuart, it's Hettie. There's a body buried on the top of Uncle Roscoe's grave in the old cemetery. I think it's a woman. And there's a car parked on the road that looks like it's been there a day or two." There was silence at the other end. "Stuart?"

"I heard you. Don't touch anything. I'm on my way."

Hettie had the distinct feeling that when he did say more, it wouldn't be something she particularly wanted to hear.

"I need a cuppa," Mrs. Braxton all but whispered. They headed back down to the car.

Stuart must have been out somewhere attending to another matter as it was twenty minutes before he arrived. She and Marlee were sitting on the back floor of Marlee's Pajero, legs dangling, the hatch raised. The Mrs. B's were facing them in their folding chairs. They all had mugs of tea in their hands. Hettie would have preferred coffee in hers, but she wasn't complaining. A plate of cake crumbs was on the floor of the car between them.

Hettie saw the look of incredulity on Stuart's face at the sight, as he pulled up behind them and got out of his police car. At least he hadn't used the siren, but the blue light was flashing.

"Don't say anything, Stuart," Hettie warned him. "We needed a little comforting. And no, I'm sorry, but there's no tea left. Can we just get on with this now?"

Stuart nodded. "All right. You can show me what you've found. The rest of you stay here. I'll need to talk to you."

Hettie walked up the slope again for the third time, and for the third time, the crows cawed and flew into the trees when they reached the cemetery, except this time there seemed to be more of them.

It only took a moment for Stuart to take in the scene before pulling out his phone. Hettie turned and walked a little way down the slope. She found a clear spot among the tussocks, and sat, legs stretched out before her. She imagined Stuart phoning in a report and arranging for a forensic team, taking photos, and scanning the area for anything that might be considered evidence. It was all of ten minutes before he joined her.

"What do you know about this?" he asked, hitching up his trouser legs and squatting beside her. He was a solidly built man somewhere in his forties, a few inches taller than her, his dark hair already peppered with grey. Hettie found his presence comforting, though she knew he could also be intimidating.

"Absolutely nothing," she replied.

"So why are you here? I can't imagine this is your usual spot for afternoon tea."

"No, the afternoon tea was the Mrs. B's idea to occupy their time while Marlee looked over the cemetery."

"Marlee being the fourth person at the tea party, I take it. Why don't you start at the beginning, Hettie? I hate having to guess what questions to ask."

Hettie leaned forward and put her head in her hands for a moment before looking up again.

"Sorry, Stuart. This wasn't the way the afternoon was supposed to go."

"No, I don't suppose it was. Neither of us are comfortable with murder despite being involved in more than we'd care for in recent times."

Hettie considered for a moment about asking his opinion on the possibility of those recent deaths being a result of trouble in the universe involving a particular character in Norse mythology, as per one Janelle Rice, but decided immediately that it would make her look more than a trifle mad.

He hadn't reacted well to previous indications of something supernatural, including a cat who understood human speech. And just what would Ceefer make of all this, in any case? Not that it mattered. This murder really did have nothing to do with her, or the Parkes in general.

"Do the police who investigate murders ever get used to it?" she asked instead.

"They follow a process and do their best to figure it out," Stuart said after a moment. "But no. They don't get used to it. At least the majority don't. Now, getting back to the matter at hand, why were you here?"

Hettie told him, starting with the phone call from Marlee. He took notes as she talked.

"Why did she ring you?" he asked when she'd finished. "What is your connection?"

"Oh, we studied teaching together, but then Marlee didn't care for it after a few years, so she went back to university and did library and history studies. She's working at the State Library now, in the Battye. We caught up again a few months ago when I took her some letters and a newspaper article I'd found. She's documenting the old cemeteries in the state. You know, the private ones on cattle and sheep stations and the like where people were buried years ago, and this one is on Parke Trust land so, she phoned me."

"I see. Thanks, Hettie. I need to talk to the rest of your group now, before the team arrives."

He stood, letting out an 'oomph' as he did so. Hettie got to her feet as well, taking care not to groan or 'oomph' as well in the process.

Back down on the road, Stuart took each of them aside for an interview. His shortest interview was with Mrs. Bronson, as she hadn't been up to the cemetery, but Hettie imagined he needed her corroboration of the why and how. He spent the most time interviewing Marlee.

Chapter 3

"Honestly," Marlee complained, as she drove them back into Woody Lake, "you'd think I was the killer returning to the scene of the crime, the way he kept questioning my motive for being there today. It's your fault I was, anyway, Hettie."

"Oh, really? Why is that?"

"I finally got to take a closer look at those letters and the newspaper article you'd brought me some months ago. You remember them?"

Hettie said she did, of course, having just explained it to Stuart. Now she had to explain to the Mrs. B's, who hadn't heard about Hettie's find amongst her grandmother's old papers. The newspaper article had reported the drowning of the two young Mason boys in the Cygnet River in 1904, and the letters, dated a few years later, were from a woman in England, writing to her sister Rhona Leadworth, who lived at the Cygnet River cattle station.

"I know the name Leadworth," Mrs. Bronson said. "But not Mason. Are they connected?"

"Not that I know of," Marlee told her. "But those little boys would be buried in that cemetery. It's what drew me there today. I'll need to come back and take more photographs and map the site at some time. At least I can do that here. Most of these cemeteries are hundreds of kilometres away. I've applied for some grant money to visit several sites in the far north."

"How exciting," Mrs. Braxton said. "It's like exploring."

Marlee gave a strained laugh. "Pretty much."

Hettie thought Marlee must be excited about her research project but was talking to cover the shock at what they'd just discovered. When they arrived back on Old Dairy Road, Hettie helped the Mrs. B's unload themselves and their goods. Marlee remained in the car, seemingly impatient to be off.

"Marlee, are you okay?" Hettie asked, leaning in at the window, her hand resting on the car roof. "You can stay overnight if you don't feel like driving home. You've had a shock. Are you going to be on your own tonight?" She didn't know if Marlee had anyone to be going home to at the moment.

"Oh, no. It's okay," Marlee assured her. "I'm living with my mum right now. She'll be expecting me. She needs company since Dad died. She gets depressed easily. We can be miserable together tonight." She gave another shaky laugh.

"Well, if you're sure. Drive carefully then. And call me if you need to talk."

"I will, thanks Hettie." Hettie stepped back and watched her friend drive off.

"Nice girl," Mrs. Braxton commented. Hettie nodded.

"I suppose they'll know who she was by now," Mrs. Bronson said thoughtfully, obviously referring to the dead woman.

Stuart had been checking the abandoned car when they left. A phone call to headquarters giving the registration number would soon provide him with the name of the person who owned it. It would be another item for the forensic team to go over when they finally arrived. She wondered if they'd get the body out before dark, picturing them sifting through the soil for any evidence as they carefully uncovered her. She shivered.

"Are you all right, Hettie?" Mrs. Braxton asked.

"None of us are all right at the moment, Edith," Mrs. Bronson snapped. "A woman's been murdered, and we found her."

"You need to go in and rest, Ila," Mrs. Braxton told her. She picked up the afternoon tea basket and one of the folding chairs and walked up the path to her front door.

"Can I help you with anything?" Hettie asked into the uncomfortable silence that followed.

"Only if you have a new hip you can spare me," Mrs. Bronson said bitterly.

"I'm sorry. Health problems can be confronting," Hettie said gently, having no real experience of it herself as yet. "Have you a date for your operation?"

"I haven't agreed to have it yet," came the snappy reply.

"No? Have you talked to your doctor about it? It's only natural to be concerned about what to expect."

"Hmph." Mrs. Bronson turned and made her way carefully down her garden path and into her own house.

Hettie watched until she was safely inside. She heard Mrs. Braxton's door open and saw the woman standing there looking out. Hettie picked up the folding chair Mrs. Bronson had left behind and joined Mrs. Braxton. The woman had tears in her eyes. Hettie leant the chair against the wall and hugged her.

"I don't know what to do," Mrs. Braxton said, pulling a tissue from her sleeve and swiping at her eyes. "I've tried being patient but she's so angry with life right now."

"I just suggested she should speak to her doctor for more information. She didn't receive it well. I'm sure she must be scared."

Mrs. Braxton nodded. "I know I would be. This is the first thing that's happened to remind us that we're actually getting older. She's having trouble accepting it."

"I can imagine."

"I'll check on her in the morning. And thank you for taking us to visit the cemetery today, Hettie. I know Ila appreciates it too."

"Despite the outcome."

"Despite the outcome," Mrs. Braxton agreed.

Hettie crossed the Road to the Cafe. Violet would be closing soon. They could walk home together. There was something about murder that made you crave company. She hoped the Mrs. B's would be okay. She was glad to know Marlee wouldn't be on her own, although whether she could talk about it to her mother about it, she didn't know.

"Merroow." Ceefer ran to her when she entered the Cafe. She picked him up and he bumped his nose under her chin and purred loudly when she rubbed behind his ears.

Tess looked up and grinned at her from the table where she was refilling the condiments and napkin supplies. One table was still occupied by a couple, finishing an early meal it would seem. It was her backyard neighbours, the Dunlops from Daisy Street. Henry Dunlop wobbled his fork in Hettie's direction, and she acknowledged them with a wave of her hand.

Violet came out of the kitchen having heard the door, and possibly Ceefer, and no doubt wondering who the late customer was and what they might want.

"Tell me you're not involved in this too," she said, looking from her mother to Ceefer. Hettie raised her eyebrows at her daughter in a 'please explain.'

"Dan got a call," Violet said, lowering her voice. "A body's been found at the old cemetery. Ceefer seems to think you know something about it."

"You know what they say about bad habits. They're hard to kick."

"Who was it?"

"I've no idea."

"So, you didn't recognise them? Not someone from around here?"

"I didn't see her face, Violet. Can we leave this conversation until we're at home."

"A woman," Violet mouthed. Hettie nodded and hoped Violet wasn't thinking of filling in more pages in that scrapbook she'd started after the last murder they were involved with.

Back home, over dinner of tuna and salmon fish cakes with sweet potato fries and a salad, they discussed the proposed Open Day. Violet thought a Sunday would be the best option when Hettie suggested Saturday.

"People are too busy on a Saturday, Mum."

"Are they?"

Violet popped a fry in her mouth and talked around it. "You don't work full time anymore. You can do stuff during the week while other people have to wait for the weekend. When did you last go to the hairdresser on a Saturday?" she asked, stabbing another fry.

It was true. She avoided the shops on a Saturday whenever she could.

"Anyway," Violet continued, not waiting for an answer, "if we hold the Open Day on a Sunday, I can open the Cafe and just concentrate on the visitors. Everyone is going to be there for the same thing. Any other day could upset the regulars." Hettie nodded.

"So," Violet considered for a moment, "if the Cafe concentrates on coffee and baked goods - pastries, muffins, cakes, scones - you could have a couple of food trucks that do sausages, burgers, perhaps pizza. What do you think? That way we aren't competing with one another but there's something for everyone."

"I knew I could rely on you to come up with a sensible plan," Hettie told her.

"Oh, and an ice-cream truck," Violet added.

"Of course. Three or four food trucks, max. They can take one end of the car park. Can I leave you to source them?"

"Sure, Mum."

The seven o'clock news carried a report on the discovery at the cemetery. Flood lights lit up the site as police forensics moved about, scouring the ground. The final image was of a covered stretcher being carried down the rise to a waiting ambulance.

"Merrow." Ceefer offered condolences from his spot curled up beside Hettie on the sofa.

Dan called in shortly before nine. Violet went to make coffee for the three of them after greeting him in the hall.

"Do they have a name for her?" Hettie asked as Dan dropped into an armchair in the living room. He looked tired.

"Alicia Feldhurst," Dan replied, rubbing his forehead. "Comes from Denmark, married with a daughter."

"Denmark?" No. Surely not. Belle had said the woman she was seeing today was from Denmark. Was it only this morning she'd told them that?

"That mean something to you?" Dan asked.

"I hope not." But there couldn't be two women from the south-western town interested in family history and visiting Woody Lake this weekend, surely. And why else would Alicia Feldhurst have been at the old cemetery if not for family research? Well, there could be other reasons, Hettie supposed, but she didn't believe in coincidences. Not around here, anyway. She reached for her phone. A call to Belle could provide an answer to that.

"They might disclose more on the late news," Dan said, accepting the coffee Violet handed him and gulping down several mouthfuls.

Hettie decided to wait and see if the late news revealed anything further before calling Belle. Violet perched on the arm of Dan's chair and Hettie picked up the mug Violet had put before her on the coffee table. She sat sipping her drink as Dan and Violet chatted about their day until the news came on.

Not only did the police disclose the woman's name, but they also asked for help from the public regarding her movements over the previous forty-eight hours. It was Detective Grayson Fox who fronted the camera with the request. Of course, it would be, Hettie thought. He was becoming the expert on murders in Woody Lake. She still felt the old thrill when she saw him. Would that ever stop?

She wondered if Larry and Gwen had heard the news of this murder. At least they wouldn't know she was involved, which would explain why Gwen hadn't rung, if they had heard of it. Her phone warbled. Speak of the devil. But it was Belle calling, not Gwen.

"Did you see the news tonight?" Belle asked after a brief greeting, her voice pitched a little higher than usual. "That woman they found at the old cemetery was the one I was supposed to meet today. She didn't turn up for our appointment and wasn't answering her phone. I thought she'd changed her mind or was held up somewhere. I can't believe it. Last thing I imagined was that she'd died. Talk about a shock."

"I suspected it might be the same woman," Hettie said, "when I heard she was from Denmark."

"How do you know that? It wasn't on the news. You've been talking to that Dishy Detective again, haven't you?"

"I have not. It was Violet's Dishy Dan who told me if you must know." Violet giggled, as colour rose on Dan's face. "But I know a little more, too. I was one of the people who found her."

"No. Not again. Hettie, what have you been doing?"

Hettie explained her trip to the cemetery with Marlee and the Mrs. B's.

"Listen, Belle, can I put you on speaker? Dan is here now. I'm sure he'd like to hear what you've got to say."

"Sure, why not." Hettie clicked on the button and put her phone on the coffee table.

"What's your connection to Alicia Feldhurst, Ms. Danvers?" Dan asked, after a nod from Hettie.

"Oh, call me Belle, please. It was a business arrangement." She repeated what she'd told Hettie and their friends earlier in the day. Hettie realised Dan was recording the conversation in an app on his own phone.

"So, you'd never met her?" he asked next.

"No, wouldn't know her from Adam. Or Eve anyway. Only spoke to her on the phone."

"When did you speak to her last, Belle?" Hettie asked.

"Late yesterday morning. She rang to confirm the time for our meeting today. Three o'clock. She'd just arrived at the Airbnb where she was staying. She was going to visit the cemetery, take some photos, and go through her material one last time, she told me."

Hettie knew the police would want that information but before she could say more Dan spoke again.

"Was it the Feldhurst family she was researching?" he asked.

"No, the name was Mason. Her grandmother was a Mason, and it was her story she was wanting to write about."

"The Masons?" Hettie echoed. Could this get any weirder?

"Do you know them?" Belle asked.

Hettie quickly explained how the newspaper item she'd found among her grandmother's belongings had told of the drowning of two young Mason boys in the Cygnet River.

"Would the boys have been buried in the old cemetery?" Dan asked.

"Most likely, if the family were living here at the time," Hettie said.

"That would explain why Alicia was here, anyway," Belle said. "I wonder if her family will want the story told still. I must admit to being curious. You don't suppose her death had anything to do with her family history?"

"Why, do you think she might've been about to reveal a secret that another family member didn't want told?" Hettie asked.

"It's possible."

"That cemetery is hardly a spot where someone would happen on her by accident, is it?" Dan suggested reasonably. "Someone must have known she'd be there."

"Apart from me, if you don't mind," Belle put in.

"Of course."

"Do you know if she was on her own, Belle?" Hettie asked.

"I've no idea. She didn't mention anyone."

"You'll need to tell the police about your connection. They'll be trying to put a picture together about her movements, and why she was here."

"Yes, I heard that on the news. Can't you pass it on, Hettie?"

"Even if I did, they'd still want to speak to you. Just call in at the Rosny station and tell them what you know."

"Will you come with me? Sergeant Higgins is a friend of yours, isn't he?"

Hettie supposed he was, especially lately when they seemed to bump into one another in the line of his work. She looked at the television. The late news had finished. It must be nearing ten. Was it too late to call him?

"I'll let him know you have some information and see what he wants to do about it, Belle. Okay?"

They ended their call, and Hettie sent a brief text to Stuart. He responded almost immediately, asking for Belle to come into the station at nine next morning. When Hettie forwarded the message to Belle her friend replied: "Meet you at the station at 9."

Hettie sighed and sent her a thumbs-up. So much for a quiet Sunday morning. At least it wasn't a day for the family's monthly Sunday lunch. With any luck, Callie wouldn't hear about her finding another dead body. Miracles did happen, didn't they?

Chapter 4

"Come on, Ceef. We can go for a nice walk," Hettie said after breakfast next morning. It was just after eight thirty. The sun was shining, although the air would be a little crisp, she knew. She had opted for black pants, a green and yellow knit, and her trademark yellow Skechers. Comfortable and casual. She went into the hall and took down Ceefer's blue harness from the hall stand.

"Ceefer?" she called when the cat didn't immediately come bounding after her. She stepped back into the living room, where a black ball of fur was curled up on the sofa.

"We can go for a walk in the park afterwards," she said, when he didn't even raise his head. "We might meet Sandra and Brutus." Ceefer opened an eye at this but didn't move. "Are you feeling all right?" He huffed and closed his eyes again. "Okay, I can take a hint."

She was surprised he wasn't curious about what he might hear today at the police station.

Unless he knew all about it already, of course. One could never be sure with that cat.

"He does need to go for a walk, Mum," Violet said, from the kitchen, as Hettie turned back to the hall. "He's getting fat and lazy. I'm going to have to stop people feeding him at the Cafe soon."

"Oh, I see. Perhaps we could keep him at home for a while, then," Hettie suggested.

"That's actually a good idea," Violet replied, stepping into the living room, coffee mug in hand. "Better than me growling at our customers for feeding him. They'll still sneak food to him, whatever I say."

Ceefer was wide awake now, eyeing them both balefully. Banning him from the Cafe, and tasty handouts, was about the only thing they had control over where this cat was concerned. He hadn't shown any ability to escape from the house and source his own free food. Yet anyway.

"Yooeew."

He jumped down from the sofa, complaining as he made his way into the hall. Hettie and Violet grinned at one another but didn't speak. The less said in front of a cat who understood what they said, the better.

Once outside, smart in his harness, Ceefer perked up, tail high, as he led Hettie over the

Cygnet River footbridge and along the riverside park, heading for the Rosny township. Myrtle Street on Sunday was even busier than a weekday, with families and couples out and about, enjoying the shopping and the cafes. Violet was right. Sunday was a day for relaxing and enjoying yourself, shedding the cares of the week for a while. Ceefer, as usual, drew smiles and comments as he paraded by. Hettie didn't think he'd object to the walk in retrospect. Did cats even do retrospect?

They turned off Myrtle Street and headed to the Rosny police station on the far corner. Hettie spotted Belle's little, blue electric-powered Nissan Leaf parked nearby at the kerb. Belle got out and locked the car door when she saw them approaching. Her red curls were tamed, tied back in a neat twist, and she was wearing grey pants and jacket with a soft blue shirt, and black flats. This was a toned-down Belle Danvers, all the better to be taken seriously, Hettie thought, considering she could be a suspect in the death of Alicia Feldhurst.

Hettie greeted her. "They might offer you a job, dressed like that."

Belle pulled a face. "Like I'd accept it. How are you Ceefer?" She bent and stroked his head.

"Mrow." The response was short and huffy.

"Oh, like that is it?" Belle raised her eyebrows at Hettie who just shrugged. Ceefer was still annoyed at being dragged out, it would seem

Inside the Rosny Police Station they were taken to an interview room where Stuart soon joined them. After the usual preliminaries, Belle told him of her contact with Alicia Feldhurst as he recorded the conversation.

"So, let me clarify this," Stuart said. "She told you when she rang Friday morning that she was going to the cemetery later that day?"

"That was what she told me."

"Did you go to the cemetery, Ms. Danvers?"

"No, I did not."

"What were you doing on Friday?"

"I was at home most of the day. I was working on the final draft of a memoir for a client. I had several phone calls, one from my mother and another from a prospective client. I popped out to do some grocery shopping a little before five, and I was home all evening."

"And no one to verify any of that?"

Belle shrugged. "The time of the phone calls will be on my phone, and there's sure to be

CCTV footage for when I was at the supermarket. But other than that, no, not really. I was on my own."

Stuart was watching her, full policeman's face on, as she spoke. "And yet you may be the only person who knew she would be at the cemetery, and when."

"I didn't know when, except sometime on Friday," Belle replied lightly. "I've never met the woman, Sergeant. And I know nothing of the family story she was working on, except for it being about her grandmother, whose last name was Mason. I hadn't received any material from her. She was to give that to me at our appointment on Saturday. I can't even begin to imagine what motive I could have for killing her."

"Mruff," came quietly from near Hettie's feet. Hettie didn't know if Stuart or Belle heard Ceefer confirming Belle's words. Not that Stuart, anyway, would have understood what was meant.

"You must have some idea of what she wanted you to do for her, Ms. Danvers. She can't just have hired you without some explanation."

"Please call me Belle, Sergeant. And I knew enough to take on the job. She wanted me to write up the research material she had collected about her grandmother's life. It's one of the things I do; write people's stories for them."

Sergeant Higgins' fingers tapped at the table. He seemed to be getting frustrated at the lack of information. "Do you have any idea why Alicia Feldhurst was visiting cemetery?" he asked.

"Well, I did assume it probably had something to do with her grandmother," Belle replied, "though I had no idea what the connection was at the time. Hettie added a little more to the story last night."

Stuart looked at Hettie, sitting quietly and trying to be unobtrusive.

"You know something about the woman who was killed?"

"No, Stuart, I've never met the woman, and I know even less about her than Belle, who had at least spoken to her. No, it was when Belle told me the grandmother's family name, Mason." Hettie repeated what little she knew about the tragic drowning of the Mason boys in 1904, when the raft they were on fell apart in the Cygnet River. "It's possible the boys were buried in our old cemetery. It was a long time ago, almost a hundred and twenty years."

Belle nodded. "And depending on when Alicia's grandmother died, it seems very likely there's a connection, so that would explain why she went there. Perhaps she was hoping to see the boys' graves."

"Which are little more than unidentified mounds of earth, if they are there," Hettie added. "There's half a dozen small mounds in the cemetery, none of which have a gravestone or a marker of any sort."

"I see. Alright, Ms. Danvers. We can leave it at that for the moment. I might want to speak to you again at some time, depending on what we find." Stuart turned off his phone on which he'd been recording the interview.

"Do you know yet how she was killed?" Hettie asked. She wasn't sure for a moment whether Stuart was going to answer her.

"There was evidence at the site that she'd hit her head on one of the gravestones," he said eventually, "but the autopsy will uncover any other injuries. Clearly, accident has been ruled out."

"Yes, she didn't bury herself. That's odd, don't you think? I mean, that she was buried. Did the person who killed her come with a shovel? Why? Were they planning to dig up something else there, and Alicia disturbed them?"

"Grave robbers," Belle said. "Does that even happen anymore?"

"I wouldn't have thought so," Hettie replied. "Perhaps there were stolen goods buried at the cemetery, or somewhere nearby, and Alicia disturbed the person digging it up."

"A gardener could have tools in their car boot," Belle said. "The killer may have found them and decided burying her was a good idea."

"Of course, you said yesterday she was a horticulturalist, didn't you?" Hettie said. "Interesting that they left the car if it was a simple mugging gone wrong, or an accident even. Had anything been stolen from her car?" Hettie asked. "I noticed it had been left unlocked."

"You all told me yesterday that no one touched the car," Stuart challenged, leaning forward. "So how did you know it wasn't locked?"

"We didn't touch it," Hettie replied, "but I saw you open the driver's side door as we were leaving. You know, I've just had a thought. If she'd been buried properly, she would have just ended up as a missing person case, wouldn't she? Perhaps that was the idea. Leaving the car makes sense then, doesn't it?"

"Do you think her death might have something to do with her family research?" Belle wondered.

"Why would you suggest that?" Stuart asked. "You said you didn't know anything about Alicia Feldhurst's research?"

"And I don't, but raking up the past often reveals secrets that people would rather not see the light of day. Perhaps she discovered the boys' drowning wasn't an accident, or someone's father wasn't who they thought he was."

"So do we know if anything was stolen from her car?" Hettie repeated her earlier question.

"We? What's this 'we' business?" Stuart wanted to know.

"Just trying to help, Sergeant," Hettie replied.

"You do have a habit of picking up information," Stuart admitted, "but if you uncover something useful, I expect you to tell me immediately. You will, won't you." It wasn't a question.

There was a small huff from Ceefer. "I always do," Hettie told him, as both she and Belle gave him their undivided attention.

"According to her family, there are several items unaccounted for. A watch and a necklace she would have been wearing appear to have been taken from the body. Her key for the Airbnb where she was booked hasn't been found, and her room appears to have been searched as well. A laptop and a thumb drive are also missing, and the car keys were left in the ignition."

"The thumb drive may have been meant for me," Belle told him, "if it had her research on it."

"It sounds as if she was in the wrong place at the wrong time," Hettie said. "Her death may have been accidental, but the killer then took the opportunity to try and cover it up and get what they could from it."

"Sounds like a very cool customer in that case," Stuart commented.

"It does, doesn't it?"

"You say her family have identified these items as missing," Belle said. "Does Alicia have family in Perth? I know she lives in Denmark."

"Her daughter is a master's student at UWA. We contacted the husband, and he gave us the girl's contact details, but he drove up himself last night."

"Did she identify the body?" Stuart nodded. "The poor girl," she said softly, echoing Hettie's thoughts.

There was a brief knock on the interview room door, and it opened to reveal Grayson Fox.

"A quick word please, Sergeant," he said, without a glance toward Hettie and Belle.

Stuart went out, closing the door behind him.

"I hope I don't have to repeat it all again," Belle said. "Even if he is handsome."

"Hpff."

"I thought you liked him, Ceef?" Hettie said, surprised.

"Mroff."

"On the fence? I see. I feel a bit the same way."

"Is he seeing that woman he brought to your mum's charity auction?" Belle asked.

"Anna Noble, the police sergeant? I've no idea," Hettie replied willing herself not to sound as if she cared. She didn't really. She had no intention of starting that relationship up again. It was just, well, it would have been a nice boost to her ego if Grayson had at least showed some interest in wanting to.

"Hpff."

Hettie was startled. She hadn't spoken aloud, had she? Surely that cat couldn't read minds as well. Heaven help them if that was one of his hidden talents.

"Well, you've got another admirer in this Sergeant, anyway," Belle said. "Have you noticed how he's trimmed up a bit lately? Wouldn't surprise me if he's getting ready to make his move."

"What?"

"Don't tell me you hadn't noticed how he looks at you?"

"How he… That's ridiculous."

There was a snicker from beneath the table. You too?

"And sharing information the way he did."

"He shared that with you too if you remember."

"Yes, but he didn't say 'tell the police' if you have some information to share," Belle retorted. "He said 'tell me,' remember."

"Honestly, Belle." Hettie found herself at a loss for words.

"He's a bit of a hunk himself, you know," Belle went on. "Not in the same league as Grayson, but a better choice if you're looking for something long term." She shifted restlessly in her seat. "I'm sure they make these chairs uncomfortable on purpose."

"More than likely," Hettie agreed. "Could we please change the subject now? I'd hate to think they can hear what's being said in here the way they do on police TV shows."

Belle giggled. "Oops." A few more minutes dragged by. "Have you done anything about the Open Day?"

"Vi and I settled on the food and the date," Hettie told her, glad for a safe subject. "Sunday in four weeks, trucks selling sausages, burgers and ice cream, and coffee and cake in the Cafe."

"Coffee and cake in the Cafe at the Croquet Club, with a cat called Ceefer," Belle all but sang. "It certainly has a ring to it."

Hettie laughed. "Don't repeat that in George's hearing, anyway," she warned, "Not unless you can add something about the Bowls Club in there. I'm in bad enough with him as it is."

"Burgers and balls at the Bowls Club with…? she hesitated, searching for something beginning with a 'b.'

"A big dog called Brutus?" Hettie offered.

It was Belle's turn to laugh. "Sandra Alberts would like that anyway. We could encourage people to bring a pet."

"You volunteering to clean up afterwards?"

Ceefer snickered.

"And then again, perhaps not."

They were both laughing when the door to the interview room opened again and Grayson came in, followed by Stuart.

Chapter 5

It was Grayson who took the chair on the other side of the table this time, while Stuart remained on his feet.

"Sergeant Higgins has filled me in on your interview," he said, his tone formal. "Thank you for providing that information, Ms. Danvers. I may have some more questions for you, though, Hettie, but we can leave that until later."

Belle's leg nudged Hettie's and did her best to ignore it. Grayson cleared his throat. Had he noticed the movement? She felt the warmth spreading over her face at the thought their conversation might have been overheard.

"I need to ask a favour of you, if you wouldn't mind," Grayson said, clearing his throat again. "Alicia Feldhurst's family would like to visit the cemetery where she was found, and they are also wanting to meet the person who found her. I was hoping you might be amenable to combining those two tasks, Hettie. It would be a help if you could."

Grayson was asking a favour of her in an investigation? To say she was surprised was an understatement.

"Um, yes, I guess. What is it you want me to do, exactly?"

"If you could escort the Feldhursts to the cemetery and answer any questions they may have about finding her. This isn't about you investigating the death," Grayson said. "I must stress that. This is strictly about providing a little support and help for the police, as we are stretched right now."

"I understand. If I do learn anything from them, of course, I will pass it on. Has the autopsy been completed?" If he was asking a favour, she'd milk it for all it was worth.

Grayson raised an eyebrow but answered. "It has. There was an injury to the head consistent with hitting one of the gravestones, likely the result of a fall, and a stab wound to the neck."

Someone who'd come prepared to kill or who, at least, carried a weapon of some sort.

"I'll introduce you to the victim's family members now," Grayson said, clearly feeling he'd imparted enough information.

"I would like to meet them too," Belle said. "Alicia did engage me to write her grandmother's story."

"I'll introduce you both," Grayson said. "The family members are Alicia's husband, Jackson, and their daughter Keira. They're in the waiting room."

Stuart went to fetch them. Jackson Feldhurst was a medium height, blue-eyed, blonde-haired fifty-something, with a ruddy face that spoke of an outdoor occupation. Daughter Keira must have taken after her mother as there was no resemblance to Jackson. Sadness and a sense of unreality seemed to emanate from them. It was hardly surprising.

After the introductions, it was decided that Hettie and Belle would drive to the cemetery in Belle's car, and the Feldhursts would follow in theirs. Hettie didn't have Ceefer's short leash with her, so she settled for tying off his walking leash to the seat belt fastening with just enough length for him to curl up on the seat.

"They looked numb, poor things," Belle said, as they headed out of Rosny and across the Cygnet into Woody Lake. Numb, yes. Trust a writer, ghost or not, to come up with an appropriate word, Hettie thought. "I feel awful for Alicia," she went on, "and I didn't even find her body."

"You did speak to her though, and more than once I imagine," Hettie said. Belle nodded. They turned left into Jersey Street and headed out of town. Hettie glanced behind and saw the Feldhurst's black SUV following.

"You've been involved with several nasty deaths lately," Belle said. "How do you deal with it?"

"I try to think of it as a puzzle."

"Does that work?"

"Not really," Hettie admitted.

Ten minutes later, it was a silent group that made their way up the rise to the cemetery. At least the crows had gone, but police tape hung from a tree, and another length hung over the metal railing around the Parke grandparents' graves.

Hettie didn't think there'd been enough wind since Saturday to cause that. Had some ghoulish sightseers visited? Belle collected the tape from the graves, as Hettie explained how they'd found Alicia's body, and indicated where she'd been buried. Jackson murmured a 'thank you.'

"Whose grave is it?" Keira asked.

"My aunt's second husband, Roscoe Slater," Hettie replied. "He died about six months ago."

"Someone you were close to?"

"No, not really." Keira nodded. She knelt and placed a bouquet of wildflowers on the spot.

Hettie stepped away and glanced at Belle, who nodded. They quietly made their way back down to the cars leaving the couple to grieve in private.

"Someone should have a word with the police about littering," Belle said, as she threw the ball of yellow tape onto the back seat of her car, earning a sharp retort from Ceefer. Belle apologised to him, and Hettie let him out and gave him some water.

"I don't know why they can't just roll it up and take it with them when they've finished," Belle went on, clearly on a roll herself. "You should mention it to Grayson. I mean, how difficult would it be to roll it up on their way out?"

"You've got a point, but I'll leave you to bring up the subject, if you don't mind."

They sat in the car and chatted until the Feldhursts came back down.

"Thank you for waiting," Jackson said, as Hettie and Belle got out to meet them.

"Is there anything else we can do for you?" Hettie asked.

"I want the story told," Keira said. "The story Mum was wanting to write about her grandmother. It's the least we can do for her. Would you still be available for that?" she asked Belle. "Whatever arrangement you had with Mum, we'll honour it."

"I'd be happy to do it," Belle said. "We had a contract. I can give you a copy of it, and you can decide if you want to go ahead, or there's anything you would like to change."

"No, I don't need to decide," Keira said, fiercely. "Whatever Mum arranged with you will be fine. I just want it done."

Belle nodded. "Your mother didn't have a chance to give me the material, though. The police told us a laptop and thumb drive were missing from her belongings."

"Yes. Her research was on both. The thumb drive was what she was going to give you," Keira said. "But she gave me a copy too, for safekeeping. In case her laptop got stolen, she said. She has it all up on One Drive anyway, but she didn't feel safe away from home. If only..." Her voice rose. "Do you think that's what it was? A theft that went wrong? It doesn't make sense. Did someone follow her? Why didn't they take the car? I mean...who would be out here?" She gave a wave of her hand at the empty countryside. "I'm just so mad. It doesn't make sense."

"The police are doing their best," Jackson said, seemingly helpless in the face of his daughter's anger and grief.

"I hope so. I just need to be doing something. Here." Keira pulled a small object from her pants pocket and handed it to Belle. "Here's the thumb drive Mum left with me. I hope it has everything you need."

"I'll look through it today," Belle said, taking it. Keira nodded.

"I know about the two Mason boys who drowned in the Cygnet River over a hundred years ago. Did their family live here? Were the boys buried in this cemetery?"

"Mum thought they were," Keira said. "Her grandmother was the boys' sister. One of the problems Mum told me she was having with her research was the conflicting information she'd uncovered about those early years. She hoped you'd be able to sort it out for her," she said to Belle. "A fresh pair of eyes. And because you live here, she said."

"I'll do my best," Belle told her. "But I'm not an expert on genealogy."

"I have a friend at the Battye Library who could help," Hettie said. "She was here, too, when we found your mother, so I'm sure she'd be interested. I suppose history or genealogy aren't your subjects at university?"

"No, I'm majoring in economics," Keira replied.

"What was your mother planning to do with her grandmother's story once it was written?" Belle asked. "Did she want it just for the family?"

"She was going to have it properly printed and give the required deposit copies to the State Library, as well as to the Denmark library."

"I see."

"Well," Jackson said awkwardly. "Thank you again for your help. Everyone has been so supportive. We really appreciate it."

"Yes, thank you," Keira said. "Can I give you my mobile number, Belle? We'll be staying in Perth until we can take Mum home for the funeral."

"The police should have some answers by then," Jackson said. They said their goodbyes and returned to their respective cars.

"Keira's right," Hettie said, as they headed for home. "It doesn't make sense. Are you sure Alicia came here on her own?"

"I've no idea," Belle told her. "She could have had half a dozen people with her for all I know. We should have asked Keira."

"I didn't like to be nosy. Whoever it was left the car though. If she was killed by someone who was with her, they would have driven away in it, one would imagine. It really does look as if someone were setting it up as a missing person situation."

"But the police would have found her when they'd searched the area. I mean, you did."

"We certainly did," Hettie replied, "but the person who buried her probably wasn't counting on the gases and rigor mortis resulting in her arm moving and the fingers poking through the soil. If that's what happened." The thought that Alicia may have lifted her arm in one final movement before she finally died didn't bear thinking about.

Belle shuddered. "Enough with the details."

"I wonder if it was Jackson. What if he followed her in his own car, thinking this would be a good opportunity to get rid of his wife far away from home, and make him the least suspicious?"

"Wow," Belle said, admiration in her voice. "That's not bad, Hettie. You should try writing mysteries."

"The police will look at him first, anyway. They may already have discounted him." Hettie pulled out her phone and googled Feldhurst Denmark. "There's a Feldhurst Landscaping Company in the town," she said scrolling quickly. "Jackson and Alicia are the owners. And it's a four-and-a-half-hour drive to Denmark, so a nine hour round trip, an hour, perhaps two, to do the job depending on how soon after arriving Alicia went to the cemetery."

"Probably around mid-day Friday, or early afternoon, according to the time of the phone call I got from her," Belle said. "It could be done."

"Yes, it could." She hoped for Keira's sake that it hadn't been, but the most dangerous people were those closest to you.

Belle dropped Hettie and Ceefer off at her door, promising to let her know what she found on the thumb drive Keira had given her.

Chapter 6

After seeing Violet and Ceefer off to the Cafe next morning, Hettie sat at the kitchen table with her laptop and a fresh coffee, planning to work on the details for the Club Open Day. She had a study at the back of the house, but she preferred to work in the kitchen. For one thing, it was more convenient to the kettle and the coffee jar, and for another, the bright front rooms were her favourite place in the house, looking out, as they did, across Old Dairy Road to the park and lake, the Sunny Vale Retirement Centre, and the Parke Bowls and Croquet Club

She started making out her list. Violet was dealing with the food requirements, but that was just one item for a successful event. She needed to have members available to give lessons and take visitors around the courts for a game. An exhibition match between players from the State team, to show off the skills involved and the fun you could have was always a drawcard. It gave people something to aspire to, and the realisation you didn't need to be athletic to be a top croquet player. A video of an international competition playing continually in the clubroom would draw attention to what could be achieved as well.

Then there was the opening of the new courts. She'd invite the CroquetWA president to perform that, with a suitable speech. All the other clubs would have to be informed of the event, too, and she needed to speak to George Engles as soon as possible, to get the Bowls Club involved. She added those items to her list along with a note to update the Club website, and to review the handout for potential members before sending it to the printer.

Whew. She needed Romola's help with this. If they could present a finished plan and timetable to the Committee on Thursday evening it would save a lot of to-ing and fro-ing, and time they didn't have. She tidied up her list and sent it to Romola in an email, asking for input, and any ideas on who could do what. That done, Hettie sat back. She could safely leave it with their Club secretary for the moment, efficient woman that she was.

She took the laptop back to her study and decided to print out her list for easy reference. Of course the printer was out of paper. She opened a desk drawer and pulled out a ream of printer paper. Underneath it was a green folder. Hettie looked at it, puzzled for a moment as she tried to remember what was in it.

Of course. It was the folder she – well Ceefer, really – had found in the bottom of that box from the Community Centre storeroom several months back. The box of rubbish her Grandma Florrie had saved because it contained 'important family papers.' The folder had papers relating to her mother's family, the Garcias. Hettie had put it away to look at later, not wanting any more family drama at the time. She pulled out the folder and set it on the desk while she dealt with the printer and her lists. She should give it to Callie.

Her phone rang. She looked at the screen. It was Marlee calling.

"Hettie, how are you? You wouldn't believe, but I knew that woman we found at the cemetery," Marlee greeted her when Hettie answered.

"You did? Well, I guess that's not surprising. She probably spent some time in the Battye researching her family history."

"What? No, I knew her when I was a teenager. She was a friend of Sophie's, my sister. They were at school together."

"My goodness, really?"

"I know. That theory of six degrees of separation always seems to be more like two or three in Perth. Well, it used to be thirty years ago anyway. Perth's population has nearly doubled in that time. It's over two million now."

"So, you knew Alicia Feldhurst back then," Hettie said, pulling Marlee back onto the subject. She had a habit of going off track and spouting information on a side matter.

"Yes. Of course, her name wasn't Feldhurst then. It was Alston. She wasn't a nice person, either. Always ready with a nasty comment. Sophie thought she was funny, but she wasn't on the receiving end." And you were, Hettie surmised. "I bet I know who killed her too," Marlee said. "Roddy Johnson."

"Really? Who was Roddy Johnson?"

"He was Alicia's boyfriend. Sophie's five years older than me and she had this group of friends from school who used to hang out together. At our house as often as not. Alicia, Roddy, Martin Hooper, Carolyn Brown. When Alicia and Roddy got together as a couple it split the group. Sophie liked him but Alicia got him. Lucky for Sophie, not so much for Alicia as it turned out. He was abusive and when Alicia tried to end it with him, he stalked her."

"Poor girl. How old were they at the time?"

"I would have been about seventeen, so, early twenties. Twenty-two or three I guess."

"So, what happened? How did it end?"

"Well, Alicia had restraining orders against him, but they were pretty useless, back then anyway, so she eventually escaped down south and ended up in Denmark. This was before everyone had mobile phones so it was easier to disappear back then than it would be now. I haven't seen Alicia since, but clearly, she made a life for herself there and married this Feldhurst fellow."

"How did you know that was who we found?" Hettie asked.

"Oh, Sophie told me. They'd been back in touch apparently and she knew Alicia's married name. I think she might have visited them in Denmark a few years back."

"And you think this Roddy Johnson would harbour ill will toward her after, what, thirty years?"

"Sophie told me he's been in prison for beating up a woman. It's only one step further to killing someone, even if he didn't mean to go that far."

"You need to tell the police, Marlee. Or Sophie does."

"It would be much easier if you just mention it to that police officer you called on Saturday, wouldn't it, Hettie? Stuart, wasn't it? You sounded like you were friends. He'd only have to check the police records. It should all be there. I really don't want to get involved. I mean, if Roddy Johnson finds out I told the police about him it could be me he comes after next."

"Oh, but it's okay if he comes after me, is it?" Hettie said, only half joking.

"He doesn't know you."

Hettie sighed. "Okay, I'll send Stuart a text and say a friend passed on the information. But if he insists on knowing who it was who told me, I'll have to tell him."

"You won't need to, and I'd really appreciate it if I wasn't mentioned. He'll find what he needs in the police records."

"Well, you should know all about records. So, you've recovered from Saturday then? You seemed a bit shaken up about finding the body. Not that that's surprising."

"It's bad enough I was there when she was found, but to have known her is completely surreal. I'm still not sure if I just dreamt it. But hey, I almost forgot to tell you my good news. My grant application has been approved."

"Oh, well done. So, you'll be off up north looking at more cemeteries then. When do you plan to go?"

"Not until autumn next year unfortunately. It'll be way too hot up there in a couple of months' time and I can't arrange with the stations any faster. I'll be needing them to accommodate me."

"Well, good luck with it. You deserve it after all the work you've put in."

"Thanks, Hettie. I appreciate that. Don't forget to message your policeman friend. I'll talk to you soon."

Hettie mulled over what Marlee had just told her. She supposed Alicia Feldhurst's death could fit with an angry boyfriend. He would have to have followed her or known where she would be. Stumbling onto her in that out of the way place was way too big a stretch. Had he been keeping tabs on her all these years, waiting for an opportunity? Well, it wasn't up to her to figure it out. She picked up her phone again and sent Stuart a brief text message with the information.

Thinking of Alicia Feldhurst's death reminded Hettie she hadn't seen or spoken to the Mrs. B's since Saturday. She wondered if Aunt Alice had any idea how Mrs. Bronson was doing, considering they were friends. A quick visit next door could answer that, followed by lunch at the Cafe. She ran a comb through her short dark hair and changed her shoes, grabbing up her bag on the way out.

Aunt Alice opened the door to Hettie's knock.

"Hello dear, did you need something?" Aunt Alice asked. "Eddie will be here in a few minutes. We're going to the Cafe for lunch."

"So am I, Auntie," Hettie told her, following her aunt into the living room. "I just wondered if you knew how Mrs. Bronson is doing?"

"I was hoping to see her today and find out," Aunt Alice said. "Edith is quite worried about her, but Ila will make up her own mind about the operation when she's ready."

"She's been really grumpy, though, snapping at everyone, especially Mrs. Braxton."

"Probably because everyone, especially Edith, is on her case about it. Ila can be quite stubborn when she's a mind, but no one wants to be told what they should do all the time. Not making an issue of it would be a better idea."

Hettie didn't have an answer to that, but it didn't matter as there was another knock on the front door. It was Eddie.

Hettie still hadn't quite got her head around the fact that her father's younger sister and her mother's step-nephew – the son of Callie's older step-brother – were an item these days. She thought Eddie must be in his mid-sixties. It made her smile to think of her aunt being with a younger man, even if there was only a handful of years between them.

Honourifics such as 'uncle' and 'aunt' weren't applied to the Garcias. Everyone in the family used their first names as Eddie preferred it that way, saying it was too complicated with the 'step' situation. The relationship reminded her to have a look through the material in the green folder before she handed it over. There might even be other Garcia's around that she didn't know about.

"Hettie's on her way to the Café for lunch, too," Aunt Alice told Eddie as she closed the front door behind her.

"Is it true you were at the cemetery when that body was discovered there?" Eddie asked, as they crossed Old Dairy Road and headed up the park.

"I was," Hettie said.

"You've got to stop doing that," he scolded. "It's not normal." Hettie couldn't argue with that.

"At least it's nothing to do with us, this time," she told him.

"Spoken like the wise woman that you are," Aunt Alice said. Eddie just grunted.

Violet greeted them from behind the counter as they entered the Café. Ceefer came toward them with his own welcome, which was warmly received by Hettie and Aunt Alice. Eddie, not so much. He was wary of Ceefer after their last murder adventure. Edith Braxton gave them a little wave from the table in the centre of the room. She was alone.

"Where's Ila this morning?" Aunt Alice asked, as she and Eddie joined her at the table. Hettie remained at the counter to collect her usual coffee.

"She's seeing her doctor. She didn't want me going with her today."

"Good. Hopefully, she'll come back with a date for her hip operation this time. Have you ordered?"

Hettie didn't get to hear Mrs. Braxton's response as her phone rang at that moment. She collected her coffee from the counter and took herself out into the garden to answer it.

"Hettie, it's Belle. Are you at home?"

"I'm at the Cafe," Hettie said, seating herself at a table in the barely warm sunshine. In two months' time they'd be seeking shade.

"I've read everything on the thumb drive Keira Feldhurst gave me and I wanted to talk to you about it. Do you have some time today?"

"Would right now suit? You could join me for lunch."

"Oh, great. I'm on my way."

Chapter 7

Hettie went back into the Cafe and let Aunt Alice know she would be having lunch with Belle. The booth in the front far corner was free and a perfect spot for a private conversation. She snagged it, and ten minutes later Belle joined her there. Tess, her hair in three shades of green today, took their order.

"It's a bit of a mess," Belle said, launching straight in. "The bottom line is that Alicia Feldhurst was questioning her grandmother's parentage. Her grandmother's name was Lily Mason Leadworth according to her birth certificate, but her father's name is given as Mason. Hardly surprising that Alicia found it confusing. But she was also questioning the parentage of her own mother, Ruby Alston, who was Lily's daughter."

"That does sound like some sort of identity crisis."

"It does, doesn't it," Belle agreed. "I'm afraid Alicia seems to have been a bit scrappy in the approach to her research, and not as thorough as I would have liked. I know Keira said her mother wanted fresh eyes on it, but what it needs is further research. Alicia needed to talk to people and not just rely on the paper records. They need fleshing out for a start. Unfortunately, the further back you go the fewer people there are still alive who can tell you what went on. And then of course, not all records still exist, for one reason or another."

"Very true," Hettie agreed, remembering her own family research not so long ago. And that green folder. "What are you planning to do?"

Belle opened her bag and took out a thumb drive that she pushed across the table to Hettie.

"I'd like you to read it, see what you think. And then we can discuss it. I've written up a timeline you can print out, to refer to while you read. It will help put things in place."

Hettie looked more closely at her friend. "I'm not an historian, Belle. I'm a primary school teacher. Are you sure I'm the right person to be looking into this?"

"Oh, yes."

"You're up to something."

"I don't want to put ideas in your head."

"You already have. You've mentioned questions about parentage."

Belle leaned forward across the table. "You know what I said when Stuart was interviewing me, about the possibility Alicia's death had something to do with her family research?"

"I do remember you mentioning it, yes."

"Well? What if it does?"

Hettie looked at the thumb drive in front of her. "You should give this to the police then, shouldn't you? Remember what Stuart said? He expects us to pass on anything we might uncover."

"Except we haven't uncovered anything yet. It's all just conjecture on Alicia's part. And you've already solved three murders, Hettie. If anyone can pick holes in this, you can."

Tess arrived with their lunch.

"I wasn't planning on investigating this death, Belle," Hettie said, when their plates were in front of them, and Tess had left.

"But you were putting forward suggestions when we talked to Stuart," Belle countered.

"That was just exercise for the mind. I told you, I try to treat it as a puzzle. I don't really want to be involved in another murder. The ones I've been part of in the past have been related to my family. Or me, in the case of Craig Lewis."

"But we don't have to deal with the murder," Belle explained. "We can just treat this as a puzzle, like you said. A puzzle involving Lily Mason's story. There's no proof this has anything to do with Alicia's death. And whatever we find we can pass on to the police, or to Stuart, as he said," she added cheekily. "That shouldn't be a problem for you, should it?"

Hettie gave her friend a narrow-eyed look. "Mmmh. Just how much genealogy research have you done?"

"The odd bit, here and there. I don't just ghostwrite the stories people give me. I sometimes need to take on pieces of the research when their stories are a bit thin. Or give them ideas on how to fill it out. I've dabbled in lots of different subjects."

"Okay then, I'll read it, and we can discuss it. And then, we'll turn it over to Stuart."

"Sure," Belle said, tucking into her Caesar salad. Hettie slipped the thumb drive into her bag.

Back home, Hettie inserted Belle's thumb drive into her laptop and watched as a list of files appeared on the screen. Research notes, newspaper clippings, a Post Graduate essay, list of references, various certificates of birth, death, and marriage, and the timeline Belle had written. There was also a file titled 'Questions.' After printing Belle's timeline, she read through it.

> *18 November 1904 – Oliver Mason, 8 years old, and Charles Mason, 6 years old, drown in the Cygnet River*
>
> *23 March 1905 – Poppy Mason, mother of the two boys, dies giving birth to a daughter. Birth certificate gives child's name as Lily Mason Leadworth. Father Chester Mason. [Note: Locate Poppy Mason diary 1900-1905]*
>
> *Lily grows up at the Cygnet River cattle station, owned by Leadworth family (Rhona and Dave).*
>
> *1919 – Lily Mason (14) working as a house servant at a boarding house in Hay Street, East Perth.*
>
> *1928 – Lily marries Arthur Winston, gardener.*
>
> *1930s – Lily and Arthur working for Sandridge family in Dalkeith.*
>
> *23 August 1940 – Arthur killed by a falling tree on the Sandridge property.*
>
> *6 October 1940 – Lily gives birth to a daughter, Ruby Rose Winston.*

Lily appears to continue working for the Sandridge family.

10 July 1966 – Ruby Winston marries Don Alston.

27 May 1969 – Ruby gives birth to Alicia May Alston.

17 December 1971 – Ruby and Don Alston die in a motor vehicle accident.

1970s – Lily and granddaughter Alicia are living in Caversham Road, West Swan.

Alicia attends West Swan Primary School and Perth Modern High School.

12 June 1984 – Lily Mason dies, age 79. Alicia is 15.

Well, that seemed clear enough. Lily Mason - born, lived, died. Hettie went quickly through the newspaper clippings relating to the death of the Mason boys, which she had seen before having given a copy of it to Marlee several months back. The article on the inquest was new to her. It added two more names. Warren and Theodore Leadworth were also on the raft when it fell apart but they survived. No blame was attributed. They must have been Rhona and Dave's children.

The various birth, death, and marriage certificates confirmed the dates in the timeline. That left the list of references and the Post Graduate essay. Hettie was intrigued to know what else a student had found to write about based on Lily Mason's rather sad life. Opening the pdf file, she found several pages photocopied from a bound volume of final assignments written by students in the 2014 Post Graduate Diploma of Public History at Murdoch University.

The essay, titled 'A Mother Mourns' was written by a Kendall Philpott. It referenced the newspaper articles on the Mason boys and included a heartbreaking collection of diary entries written by their mother Poppy Mason. The quoted diary entries were all about loss, grief, and hopelessness, and a marriage falling apart. The essay ended with the date of Poppy's death in March 1905 from a broken heart, and the disappearance from the district of her husband Chester.

She found it surprising that the diary entries made no mention of the new life Poppy was carrying. Even a comment such as, what was the point of bringing a life into the world when it could be taken so easily, or something about the hope that a new life could bring. On consideration, she decided that Kendall

Philpott had a highly developed sense of drama and had simply not quoted anything positive from Poppy's diaries, presuming of course, it had been there.

She could also understand why Alicia had become suspicious when there was no mention of Poppy's pregnancy, and why she had begun to doubt that Poppy Mason was her great-grandmother. The name Leadworth on her birth certificate was an added red flag.

Hettie opened the reference list and found the entry for Poppy's diary.

Diary of Penelope (Poppy) Mason, Cygnet River Station, 1900-1905, Battye Library of West Australian History, Private Archives, MN 2-612. (Can't locate)

So the diary was missing? Or perhaps it had been misplaced in the collection. It could happen if a researcher had several items out at the same time. Hettie was curious now as to where Alicia, then aged fifteen, had ended up when Lily died. Perhaps she had been sent to a foster home, or had a family friend taken her in? Had the upheavals of her childhood prompted her to learn about her family history, and in the process begin to question who she really was? A missing reference as important as a diary would undoubtably add to her concerns.

"**I**'ve read through all the material Belle," Hettie said, her phone on the kitchen counter as she put together a salad to go with the shepherd's pie Violet had promised for dinner that evening. "I'm not sure what to make of it, to be honest."

"Oh." Hettie could tell she was disappointed.

"I can sort of understand Alicia's suspicions, though," Hettie said. "Poppy Mason's diary could offer some light on the subject of Lily's parentage, if it can be found."

"Yes, because Lily could be the child of Poppy Mason and a Leadworth, given what her birth certificate says."

"I find that really odd," Hettie said, chopping the end of a cucumber. "I'm not sure how you can give a child a different name to that of its parents on a birth certificate. Perhaps the Leadworths adopted her after Poppy died."

"We really need to find that diary, but it seems to be missing from the Battye Library collection."

"I can give you my contact at the Battye who might be able to help. You know, I did read somewhere that it's considered one in every five references in a thesis is incorrect."

"Well, if the diary references in this essay are wrong it would mess with that theory, seeing as the diary forms practically the basis for the whole story."

"I'd place a bet on that MN number being written wrongly in the first place and then copied and pasted all the way through the essay. What if the dash is supposed to be a number, or the dash shouldn't be there at all, or one of the other numbers is wrong? Shouldn't be that difficult to check the options."

"All right, Miss Marple," Belle said. "We'll have to chase that up. Moving on to the later question mark in Lily's timeline. In 1940, after Lily's daughter Ruby is born, she continues to work for the Sandridges. How does that sit?"

"It's unusual. A housekeeper with a new baby. Her employers would have to be incredibly accommodating."

"Unless the baby's father was a Sandridge," Belle said.

"Mmm. Or the child could have been put into an orphanage," Hettie countered, as she tore up the lettuce leaves, "and Lily could have paid for her to stay there until she was old enough to be useful. Not much choice for a woman on her own with a child in the forties, you realise."

"Okay, all those things are possible, but I can't write a story about what-ifs. I need to talk to people."

"But both these parentage questions go back a long way, Belle. Eighty years, a hundred and twenty years. No one is alive who knows what happened back then."

"Someone who is a hundred years old could know what happened eighty years ago," Belle argued. "But I know, it's unlikely. And it may be that we can't give everything a black and white answer."

"You do know, a DNA test would solve both those issues."

"Yes, but only if the people involved agreed to have one, right? Alicia spoke to Cynthia Bailey – she's Warren Leadworth's daughter – but only in a phone call. The Bailey's live in the Valley and own one of the vineyards and restaurants there."

"So do the Sandridges," Hettie said. "At least one of the younger family members has a business there."

"Yes, they do. Anyway, I wanted to ask if you'd come with me to speak to Cynthia Bailey."

"Oh? Why do you need me to come with you?"

Belle hesitated. "Well, there has been a murder, hasn't there? All the mystery and crime shows you see on TV make it clear you shouldn't go snooping around on your own."

"Are we snooping about a murder? I thought we were checking up on family research."

"What if one of those families, the Leadworths or the Sandridges, are part of Alicia's family tree after all? And what if one of them was afraid that Alicia could be about to claim a share of what they have? Neither of those two families are poor. That's a motive for murder, isn't it?"

Hettie couldn't argue with that.

Chapter 8

"Turn our backs on you for five minutes and you're off finding dead bodies," Gwen said, exasperation at a high level. "How in heaven do you do it?"

Hettie handed her sister-in-law a glass of red wine and poured one for herself.

"As long as finding other people's bodies is all she does," Violet said, putting plates and cutlery on the dining room table. There was lasagne in the oven and Hettie's green salad on the counter awaiting its dressing.

Hettie gave Gwen a look. See what you've done now? You've worried Vi. Gwen took a sip of wine and kept silent.

"She wasn't on her own, though, Vi," Larry said. "Apparently three other people were there too."

"You seem to know a lot about it," Hettie said. "And if anyone is counting, it's actually the only body I've found. Other people found the other bodies."

"You just got involved in finding the killer."

"I'm not involved in finding this one."

"Mruff."

"See? Ceefer knows I'm not involved."

Gwen eyed him suspiciously. "We know a bit about it because we were in Denmark on Sunday," she said. "It was the talk of the town."

"Good. You need to tell the police what you learnt then. Now tell us what else you did on your holiday. Did you go on the tingle treetop walk? Are the wildflowers out yet? Do you want dinner?"

Fortunately, Gwen could take a hint, especially when it was delivered strongly enough. Five minutes later they were joined by Aunt Alice, Elly and Rafe and the girls.

Over dinner the conversation was about holidays, and viewing the plethora of photos Gwen and Larry had taken with their phones. When that topic was exhausted, Hettie told them of the planned Open Day at the Club.

"That sounds like fun, Mum," Elly said. "Do you want any help? I could design some posters."

"I hadn't even thought of that," Hettie said. "Could you do them by the end of the week, though? I have handouts going to the printers. The posters could get done at the same time."

"Sure. I just need the dates, and the details of what's happening."

"I'll send that to you now," Hettie said, pulling out her phone.

"We can put a poster up in the office," Gwen offered.

"And in the Cafe, of course," Vi said.

"I'm putting an advert in the *Record*, too," Hettie said, looking up from the text message she was sending Elly. "Could you design that for me as well, Elly?"

"Sure, Mum."

"Make sure you let Jack and Mum know about it," Larry said, spearing another olive. "And Pearl and Max. They won't hear about it through croquet channels, and they'll feel you're not keeping them in the loop if they learn of it through an advertisement or a poster."

Larry was right. This recent murder had distracted her, despite not really being involved in it.

"Oh. I just had a thought," she said now. "I was going to have our CroquetWA president open the new courts, but do you think I should ask Dad or Callie to do it?"

"Now, that is a good idea," Gwen said. "I vote for Callie."

"Definitely," Larry agreed.

"Grandma loves to be the centre of things," Elly put in.

"Yes, she certainly does," Aunt Alice murmured.

Well, you couldn't please everyone, Hettie thought. She made a mental note to call on her mother next day and deliver the invitation in person. And to update her list of things to do. And talk to Romola. She hit send for her text message to Elly. That was done anyway.

Everyone left for their respective homes shortly after. Well, almost everyone. Gwen and Larry lingered.

"No more evasion. I want to hear everything that's been going on," Gwen said.

Hettie sighed. There seemed to be no getting around it. She spent the next twenty minutes describing finding the body, talking to the police on Sunday, talking to the Feldhursts, talking to Belle, and talking to Marlee. What she didn't say was what she and Belle were going to be doing tomorrow. Gwen was just as likely to want to join in and Hettie couldn't see how that would be a good thing, because they weren't investigating the murder. They were investigating the family history.

"So, what did you hear down in Denmark?" Hettie asked instead.

"We heard quite a few comments about the big bad city," Gwen said, "and how this would never have happened if she'd stayed at home. But there was also an undercurrent that hinted she probably brought it on herself. I got the feeling Alicia Feldhurst wasn't the most popular person in town."

"Oh, in what way?"

"We were there for barely twenty-four hours, you know. We didn't have time to get her whole life story. But I heard one person say Jackson might enjoy life a little more with his wife gone."

"Most men probably feel that way at some point," Larry put in, very unwisely.

"Did you hear anything?" Gwen asked, putting a hand to her ear.

"Not a thing," Hettie said. "Anyway, the police will be checking on Jackson. His credit cards might show evidence of petrol bought on the day. Or he was having an affair and getting rid of Alicia was less expensive than a divorce. They do have a business together. Anyway, I'm not investigating."

"Says you."

"Merroow." Ceefer lifted his head and glared at Gwen.

"What did I say?"

"I don't think he likes this murder," Hettie said. "He doesn't seem to want anything to do with it."

"Mruff."

"Okay. I get the message, Ceef," Hettie soothed. "And despite what Gwen thinks, I'm not investigating."

"I'll want a full reporting during the week," Gwen said, as Hettie saw her and Larry out at the back door.

"You'll be disappointed then," Hettie replied. "There won't be anything to tell."

She could still hear Gwen laughing as she and Larry crossed Elly's backyard to their own.

Belle's little electric car purred down West Swan Road next morning past vineyards, horse paddocks, wineries, farm buildings converted to restaurants, purpose-built eateries, wedding venues, and small groupings of retail premises that serviced them all, some looking more prosperous than others. And lots of open space and blue sky. Belle had made an appointment for ten o'clock to speak to Cynthia Bailey.

"So, no questions about alibis, or whereabouts, or motives for Alicia's murder. We can discuss it if they raise the matter, but no accusations," Hettie was saying. "We're investigating Lily Mason's life not her granddaughter's murder."

"Absolutely," Belle agreed. "And here we are at Bailey's Bistro."

A grey Commodore was just pulling out of the driveway of the Bailey property as they slowed to enter the place. Hettie only saw the back of the driver's head, as he turned in the opposite direction, heading toward Perth, but she was sure it was Grayson's car.

The police must be following up on Alicia's contacts. Even if her laptop was missing, Keira had said she had her research stored in the cloud. More to the point right now, how would they be received by the Baileys if the police had just questioned them about her murder? It didn't take long to find out.

A man of middle age stood watching as they pulled up in the restaurant carpark. He scowled as Hettie and Belle got out of the car.

"We've just been questioned by the police, and now you've come to harass my mother with more stupid questions," he said, without waiting to ascertain if they were who he thought they were.

"Hello. I'm Belle Danvers," Belle told him politely. "Your mother agreed to talk to me.

We have nothing to do with the police and we've no intention of harassing anyone."

"Just make sure you don't, or you'll answer to me. She's in the house." He indicated a building at the far end of the car park, partly obscured by a screen of bottlebrush and grevillea shrubs, green but not yet in flower.

"Alicia mentioned Cynthia's son, Leighton, in her research," Belle said, as she and Hettie made their way down the car park, and around the edge of the garden to the front door of the house. "That must be him. A murder suspect, do you think?"

"The police must think so," Hettie said. She hadn't looked behind, but she was sure he'd watched them walk away based on the prickling on the back of her neck.

"So, just as well we're not investigating a murder, then," Belle said. "We're just gathering information about a family history."

Which hopefully hadn't led to murder, Hettie wanted to say but didn't. Belle's knock was answered by a harried-looking woman in her fifties who opened the door to them.

"You won't upset her, will you?" she said, when Belle introduced them both. "I've just got her settled again after that policeman finished with her. Why they thought we'd know anything about that woman's death, I don't know. We'd never even met her."

"We certainly won't upset her on purpose," Belle assured her.

"I suppose that's as much as one can expect these days," came the mumbled reply. "I'm Marion, by the way, Leighton's wife. Cynthia's my mother-in-law." Hettie and Belle nodded acknowledgement.

Cynthia Bailey proved to be a small stick of a woman in a wheelchair. She could have been a hundred, but Hettie knew from Alicia's research she was in her mid-eighties. One thing was certain. She hadn't been hanging around a cemetery waiting to kill Alicia Feldhurst. She looked as if a slight breeze would blow her away. If she was involved, someone else had done the deed for her.

"I hope you two will be able to understand what I tell you about Lily Mason," Cynthia said in a thready voice, when Belle and Hettie had introduced themselves again, and were seated on the sofa near her wheelchair. "Because that Alicia woman didn't seem to when I spoke to her." She coughed.

"Do you need your throat lozenges, Ma?" Marion asked.

Cynthia waved her hand. "No, no. Fetch us some tea. You'll have tea, won't you." Hettie didn't feel she could ask for coffee when Belle simply said, yes, that would be lovely. "I missed my earlier cup because of that policeman. I wasn't offering him anything, asking all those impertinent questions about where everyone was on Friday, and what they were doing. Now," she said, as Marion left the room to attend to the tea, "I can't give you much time after that earlier visit. My energy runs out quickly these days."

"We appreciate whatever time you can give us," Belle assured her.

"Yes, well, what you need to know is that Lily Mason was not a Leadworth, despite the name on her birth certificate, courtesy of my grandmother, Rhona. When Lily's mother died giving birth to her, Rhona took the baby in and raised her. Not that she got any thanks for it, mind."

"So Poppy Mason died in childbirth," Belle clarified.

"That's what I just said. She'd already lost her two boys, and she was exhausted with grief and hopelessness, according to Rhona. Chester Mason blamed Dad for the accident too, though he was only twelve himself at the time, but it was his raft that fell apart. My father was plagued with nightmares about that day for the rest of his life. Chester never wanted anything to do with Lily. Reminded him of Poppy she did. He left the Station after Poppy died, and no one ever saw him again."

"Did the Leadworths adopt Lily?" Hettie popped the question in quickly as Cynthia paused to wipe her mouth with a tissue.

"Not officially. This was a long time ago and they were a long way from the city back then. She's probably lucky her birth was registered, but life would have been difficult for her later if it weren't. No, Rhona thought it would save a lot of trouble if Lily was a Leadworth, but at least she put Mason in there as well. I think, really, she was afraid they'd take the baby away and put her in some orphanage."

"So, Lily knew she wasn't a Leadworth?" Belle asked.

"Eventually. It's why she ran away." Cynthia raised her voice. "Marion, where's that tea?"

Chapter 9

"It's just coming, Ma," Marion called appearing at that moment with a tray with teapot and cups which she placed on the low table in front of them. She poured a cup and placed it on the little table attached to Cynthia's wheelchair.

"She ran away?" Belle questioned, accepting a cup from Marion with a thank you.

"That's what I said," Cynthia replied, taking up the biscuit Marion placed on the edge of her saucer. "Someone told her she wasn't a Leadworth, and when she asked Rhona about it, and learnt who she really was, she ran off to the city. Although Perth could barely be called a city back then."

"That would have been around 1919," Belle confirmed.

"Something like that." Cynthia dunked the biscuit in her tea and just got it to her mouth before it fell apart.

"Did you know Alicia Feldhurst was going to be at Woody Lake at the weekend?" Hettie asked.

"No, why should I?" Cynthia replied, mopping biscuit off her chin with a tissue. "I've only spoken to her once, on the phone, and that was months ago. What sort of story is she writing about Lily anyway?"

"Well, it's basically Lily's life story," Belle said. "I can give you a copy of the timeline I drew up from her research." Belle drew a sheet from her folder and handed it to Cynthia. Marion moved to stand beside her mother-in-law to read it with her. There was murmuring as they pored over it.

"Look, Ma," Marion said pointing. "Sandridges. Do you think Lily was just down the road all that time?"

Hettie and Belle exchanged a quick glance. "We thought she was working for the Sandridges in Dalkeith," Hettie said.

"The old lady lived in Dalkeith," Cynthia said, "but one of the boys, Matthew, lived here in the Valley. His son, James, has the place now. James and Tina. It's the same as ours, vineyard, and restaurant. I think they have some cabins they rent out, too. Or at least they used to. The Sandridges had a finger in a lot of pies, back in the day, but it's the grandchildren who run it all now."

"I'm hoping to talk to the Sandridges about Lily," Belle said.

"Good luck with that," was Cynthia's murmured comment. Interesting. Hettie didn't think the Sandridges were standoffish. Was there a bit of competition between the two families regarding business?

"Alicia also mentions a diary in her research. It belonged to Poppy Mason, and it covered the time the boys drowned, but Alicia hadn't been able to find it. Do you have it, or know anything about it?"

"Poppy Mason's diary?" Cynthia repeated. "I seem to remember Alicia asking about that too. Where did that idea come from? When Poppy died and Chester left, Rhona cleared out their cottage and saved the papers she found there. There wasn't much. She left the papers with Dad. If Rhona found a diary, she didn't pass it on to him because I saw everything there was. I have it all now."

"You do? May we see them?" Belle wanted to know.

"Marion, hand me that folder on the table," Cynthia told the woman. Marion picked up a thin, buff-coloured manila folder from the dining table on the other side of the room and handed it to Cynthia who held it out to Belle.

Belle took the folder and opened it. Inside were the marriage certificate of Penelope Walters and Chester Mason, dated 12 February 1897; birth certificates for the two boys, Oliver, and Charles; and a sheet showing that Poppy, Chester, and Oliver travelled from Liverpool to Australia in 1901 on the *SS Runic*.

"But no diary?" Hettie asked.

Cynthia shook her head. "Rhona lived here with us for the last ten years of her life. She never made any mention of a diary in my hearing, though I was only a child at the time. Perhaps she'd given it to Lily many years ago. That would make sense, wouldn't it, if it was her mother's diary?"

Belle and Hettie had to agree it would, though Hettie wondered why Rhona wouldn't have given Lily all the papers relating to the Mason family, but then thought it might have been because they were official documents, and Rhona had felt they would be safer with her.

"Rhona had a great many stories about the Cygnet River station and the people who lived and worked there," Cynthia said. "She and my grandfather moved to the city when they sold the place, but when he died, she came here.

The place was a cattle station back then, before it went to sheep, and then dairy cows. Not that she was around to see all that. She remembered it as it used to be."

"Did Chester Mason work for the Leadworths?" Hettie asked.

Cynthia nodded. "Parke was your name, wasn't it?" she asked Hettie now. "Are you a Parke by birth, or did you marry into the family."

"Jack and Callie Parke are my parents. Do you know them?"

"I knew your grandparents. Florrie was a lovely young woman back in the day. They did well for themselves, turning that dairy farm into housing. I preferred the place as it was. We used to ride our horses over that way. I don't know why things have to change so much. The place is overrun with people these days."

Hettie couldn't help wondering how she equated her family's successful business with that idea. Without people there'd be no one to drink their wine or eat in their restaurant.

"Is your grandmother, Rhona buried in the old cemetery?" Hettie asked.

"No. Dad wouldn't go near that place. The Mason boys are buried there. Both Rhona and Dave are buried at Karrakatta."

"Is Poppy Mason buried there? There's no gravestone or marker for her. Or for the boys. Not now anyway."

Cynthia nodded. "Buried next to her boys, she was. They only had wooden crosses to mark the graves. You could still see them seventy-five years ago. My grandmother took me there when I was about eight years old. It's the only time I've been to the cemetery, though we used to ride through the area a lot later on. Rhona had stories about everyone buried there."

"Do you remember them? The stories?" Hettie asked, thinking Cynthia might be a useful source of information for Marlee.

"I do, but really only because of the photo."

"There's a photo of the cemetery?" Belle asked.

"My grandmother took it the day she took me there. It's in the pocket in the back of the folder."

Belle turned the folder over and opened the back cover. The edge of the pocket was cleverly hidden along the fold. Inside was a tiny, faded, Kodak Brownie photograph of the cemetery showing Cynthia, an unhappy-looking eight-year-old, standing beside graves marked with timber crosses that no longer existed.

"I was standing near Poppy's grave," Cynthia said. Belle took several photos of the photograph with her phone. Hettie wondered if the image could be enhanced enough to be of use.

"Did Rhona talk about the Mason boys and how they'd drowned?" Belle asked.

"It wasn't Dad's fault," Cynthia almost shouted, slapping her knee.

"Ssh, sshh." Marion was quickly beside her. "Don't upset yourself, Ma." She sent a warning look to Belle and Hettie.

"I'm sorry, Mrs. Bailey," Belle hastened to assure her. "I wasn't accusing anyone."

"Dad had nightmares all his life about that accident," Cynthia went on, distraught. "Don't you go writing it up to make it his fault those two little boys died. He was just a child himself."

Marion made more soothing noises and Cynthia calmed down a little.

"Can you tell us about it?" Hettie suggested quietly. "If Belle knows how it happened, she can make sure the story is told in the right way."

"What do you say, Mother?" Marion said. "Set the record straight?"

"I suppose I could."

"May I record it on my phone?" Belle asked. "That way it will be word for word."

Cynthia nodded and sat up a little straighter.

"There isn't much to tell. Dad — that's Warren Leadworth, Rhona and Dave's middle boy — he and his older brother had made a raft with four-gallon drums and a few boards. Dad was only twelve at the time. He, his younger brother, Teddy, and the two little Mason boys, took it out on the river one day, larking about, playing pirates, so he said.

"According to Dad, they overbalanced the raft, and it tilted, tipping them all off into the water. None of them could swim worth a stitch, but Dad managed to grab Teddy. They couldn't get back on the raft because it tilted every time they tried, and the ropes tying the boards to the drums slipped. He got them both to the bank using one of the boards that had come loose, but the two Mason boys had disappeared."

There was a little silence at the end of the story. Cynthia closed her eyes.

"Thank you," Belle said.

"Do you want to rest now?" Marion asked her mother-in-law.

Cynthia didn't appear to hear her.

"Lily visited that one time," she said, almost to herself. "Not long before Rhona died. She cried afterwards."

"I think it's time you were leaving," Marion said quietly, a minute or so later, when Cynthia seemed to have dropped off to sleep.

"Thank her for speaking to us," Belle said, when Marion walked out with them. "It was very helpful."

"Do you have anything to add to what Cynthia has told us?" Hettie asked, sensing Marion had something on her mind.

Marion stepped out into the garden, closing the door quietly behind her. "I know why Lily ran away when she did," Marion said. "Warren had come back from the War in 1919. He was twenty-six. Lily was a very pretty girl at fourteen and he was interested in her. She thought he was her brother, of course, so he had to tell her who she really was, and that it was okay for them to be together. Lily ran away in the end because Warren wouldn't leave her alone. A lot of men didn't come back from the war in a good way."

"What do you make of all that, then?" Belle asked when they returned to the car. "Was that a carefully orchestrated effort to convince us

Lily was a Mason and not a Leadworth? Or was it genuine?"

Hettie considered. "I thought Cynthia seemed genuine enough in what she told us, but that's only as far as she knows it, and that's all second-hand, isn't it? I'm wondering, now, if Lily ran away because she really was a Leadworth, and Warren really didn't come back from the war in a good way, as Marion said. Maybe that essay that's based on the diary is right, and Poppy Mason wasn't pregnant when her boys drowned."

She startled when someone rapped on the car window. It was Leighton Bailey. Hettie rolled the window down.

"I hope you're done," he said, as belligerent as before. "We don't need anyone poking their noses into our family."

"Why, have you something to hide?" Hettie asked, projecting her most innocent manner. Leighton's eyes looked about to pop. "I don't believe we've been introduced. I'm Hettie Parke."

She didn't do it very often, almost never in fact, but dropping the Parke name in the local area, where they were known, could have a positive effect on a sticky situation. Not this time.

"You should know better then, shouldn't you," he said. "And I don't need Jack Parke's patronage to run a successful business." He turned and stormed back toward the restaurant.

"I don't think I'll be welcome here any time soon," Hettie said.

Belle started the engine. "It's lunch time, and I'm hungry. Shall we go to the Cafe?"

"Is the Sandridge restaurant open for lunch on a Tuesday?"

Belle grinned. "I guess there's only one way to find out."

"I wonder if the police have visited them this morning," Hettie said as they drove further down West Swan Road.

Chapter 10

The car park at Sandridge's Valley Oasis was over half full when they drove in.

"Something smells good," Belle said, as they headed for the entrance. Hettie had been there before and wasn't surprised by the ice cream counter just inside the front door. It was the perfect spot to tempt customers for that little extra to round off their meal as they were leaving.

"How are we going to do this?" Belle asked as they chose a table on the partly enclosed patio at the side of the main room. The view was across a strip of lawn to the vineyard, stretching as far as they could see to the low hills beyond. There was no sign of leaf buds on the vines yet. The weather was still too cold.

"I don't know if any of the Sandridge family actually work in the restaurant," Hettie replied. "Let's see what we can find out first."

They studied their menus, and Hettie went to the counter to place their orders, a haloumi salad for her, and the shrimp salad for Belle.

The server was a pleasant young man with a ready smile.

"Can you tell me if any of the Sandridge family are in the restaurant today?" she asked casually, as she tapped her credit card on the card reader. "If there are," she said as he hesitated, "would you mind telling them Hettie Parke would like to say hello?"

He smiled and nodded. "Sure."

Hettie thanked him and went back to the table, telling Belle what she'd done. Perhaps her name would work this time.

"If anyone shows up, I will leave it to you to explain what you want," she said. After all, she wasn't investigating a murder, she was just helping Belle with her research.

Belle was agreeable with that. They chatted about everything over lunch, except Alicia Feldhurst and Lily Mason, and had just ordered coffee when a smartly dressed woman about their age approached the table. She looked from one to the other as she came over.

"You must be Hettie," she said looking at Hettie.

"I am."

The woman laughed. "I'm Tina Sandridge. We've not met before, but I don't know of any Parke with curly red hair, so I figured it must be you. I was told you were wanting to speak to me."

"Thank you for coming over," Hettie said. "This is my friend Belle Danvers. She's the one hoping to speak to someone in the Sandridge family. Won't you sit for a moment?"

Tina said hello to Belle and pulled out the empty chair at the table.

"How is your father?" she asked, turning back to Hettie. "I haven't seen him for several months. He and Callie used to be regulars here for lunch."

"He's fine, thank you for asking," Hettie said wondering if Callie had changed their favourite lunch venue. Fortunately, Tina didn't pursue it.

"I'm glad he's well. And what can I do for you?" she asked Belle.

Belle launched into a brief explanation of her project for Keira Feldhurst. "I'm just trying to fill in some of the blank spots in my client's notes," she said finally.

"Feldhurst. I feel that name should mean something to me."

"Alicia Feldhurst was the woman whose body was found in the old cemetery at Woody Lake," Hettie put in.

"Of course."

"Hettie found her," Belle added.

"There were four of us, but yes," Hettie agreed.

"How dreadful. And Keira is her daughter? I see," she said, when Belle nodded. "Well, I'm a Sandridge by marriage, so I can't help you much with your questions. James, my husband, probably can't tell you much either. But I do know a family member who might, and you're in luck because she's visiting us now. Kimberley is a few years older than James and knows more about the family background."

"Would she be willing to speak to us today?" Belle asked. "I could make an appointment for another day if not, but as we're here…" She let the suggestion hang in the air.

"I'll see what I can do," Tina said with a smile. "Just give me a moment."

Their coffees arrived as they waited. Then Tina was back. "Kimberley can give you a few minutes," she told them. "She'll be along shortly. I must get back to work now. It was nice meeting you, Belle. And say hello to your father for me, Hettie."

"Mmm. Something's upset her," Hettie observed as Tina hurried off. "What odds Kimberley isn't as happy to talk to us as Tina expected."

That observation was quickly evident when Kimberley reached their table. She was a tall, big-boned woman who, at the moment anyway, was exuding an attitude.

"What's all this about the Feldhurst murder? Why would you think the Sandridges would know anything about that?" she demanded, looming over their table.

"We don't," Hettie said, as Belle looked a little startled at the aggressive greeting. "We were hoping you could tell us something about Lily Mason, or Lily Winston as you may have known her by. She worked for the Sandridges in Dalkeith in the 1930s. Can you help throw any light on her life?"

"Lily Winston? It's been a long time since I've heard that name."

"You knew her?" Belle asked.

"Yes, she lived just up the road when I was growing up. She had her granddaughter living with her. They used to visit here sometimes."

"The granddaughter was Alicia. Alicia Feldhurst," Hettie said.

Kimberley stared at Hettie, mouth open. She pulled out the chair where Tina had been sitting and plonked herself down. "That's who died? Alicia Winston?" Hettie nodded. "I didn't know. Drat. I owe Tina an apology now."

"And apologies from us for any confusion," Hettie told her and nodded to Belle to take over.

"The thing is," Belle began, "Alicia had contracted me to write her grandmother's story, and now I'm doing it for her daughter, Keira." She went on to explain what little they knew of Lily's life that was relevant to the Sandridge connection. Kimberley nodded.

"Well, I can tell you quite a lot as it happens," Kimberley said, seeming to want to make up for her earlier attitude. "Lily was basically a member of our family. She worked here for years. The house she was renting when she retired belonged to us. I don't know if Dad bought it for her to live in, or if we'd always owned it. Hers was a sad story. I heard the whole of it from Mum when Lily died, but I'd picked up bits and pieces over the years. Her mother had died when she was born, her husband died when she was expecting their child, then her daughter died, and she was left to raise her granddaughter, Alicia."

"Do you know what happened to Alicia when Lily died? She was only fifteen."

Kimberley shook her head. "So was I. Or sixteen, anyway. I liked Lily, but I didn't like Alicia. She was a piece of work. I was glad she wasn't around anymore, to tell the truth. I can't say I'm all that surprised someone killed her really."

"Do you know anything about Lily's life with your family in Dalkeith, when her daughter was born?" Belle asked now.

"Ah, that's family legend, that is," Kimberley told them, nodding her head.

"We know Lily's husband died when a tree on the property fell on him," Belle prompted, when Kimberley didn't say any more.

"He wasn't the only one. My grandfather died in that accident too. Before my time of course."

"How tragic. Did Lily come here then?" Hettie asked, as Kimberley seemed to have gone off into a daydream.

"Oh, no. Sorry, I'm just trying to remember everything I've heard. It's been a while. My grandmother was much younger than my grandfather. That was often the case back then I believe."

"It was," Belle said. "A man had to be established and able to support a wife and family before he married, so he was often well into his thirties or even forties, and his wife could be twenty years younger with years of childbearing ahead of her."

Kimberley nodded. "Well, my grandmother was only thirty-two when grandfather died, and their children were still young. I think my dad was only about eight at the time. Lily stayed with Grandma, helping look after the children, and her own baby daughter Ruby. They supported one another, you know, both having lost their husbands in that accident. Then my grandmother married again and that's when Lily came here, after the end of the war, I think. My great-uncle Ronald, one of my grandfather's brothers, owned this place then. Dad took it over much later. Mum told me Lily was like an aunt to my dad and his brothers. That's why they looked after her. She was family."

How much family, Hettie wondered. Belle was wondering too.

"Was there ever any question, do you know, about whether Lily's daughter Ruby was her husband's child?" Belle asked tentatively.

Kimberley snorted. "You mean if she might have been my grandfather's child?" she said flashing a scornful look at Belle. "That was Alicia's idea, I'll bet. Typical. She envied what others had, you know? No one had a bad word to say about Lily, not that I've ever heard. My dad cried at Lily's funeral. Alicia didn't."

Belle nodded. "If Keira, Alicia's daughter, wanted a DNA test, would the family be agreeable to that, do you think?"

"Oh, good grief. Is Keira like her mother?"

"I've no idea. I've only met her the once after her mother died."

Kimberley shook her head. "I think that would have to be a family decision." She screwed up her face in concentration. "That would have made Ruby my dad's half-sister, wouldn't it? And Alicia would have been my aunt, and Keira my cousin. Any family resemblance?"

"Not with you, I wouldn't have said," Hettie told her.

"Perhaps Keira's adopted. Or Alicia was her stepmother," Kimberley said. "One can only hope. I wouldn't want to be related to someone like Alicia, but as they say, you don't get to pick your family, do you? Well, it's been... interesting... talking to you. I guess we'll hear whatever in due course."

"Oh, just one more thing, if you don't mind," Hettie said quickly, as Kimberley got to her feet. "Do you know if Lily left anything to someone in your family? There was a diary belonging to her mother. We know it existed, and we think Lily must have had it, but it's missing now. It could add a lot to the story of Lily's life if we could find it."

Kimberley shook her head. "No, sorry. I've never heard of it. I'm not sure who I'd ask about it now, either."

"It was a long shot. Thank you for your time, Kimberley. It's greatly appreciated," Belle told her.

"I don't know about you, but I'm exhausted," Hettie said, as they drove back home. "Information overload."

"I know how you feel," Belle said. "I find it surprising that Alicia didn't contact the Sandridges, though, especially as she did speak to Cynthia. I wonder if the parting with the Sandridges after Lily's death was contentious."

"Could be. She might have been hoping the Sandridges would take care of her, and they refused," Hettie said. "I'm not sure all Alicia's questions can be answered, Belle. There are lots of things that later family members never know about their parents and grandparents. At least Poppy Mason's diary is something concrete. You should concentrate on finding that."

"Good idea."

"I'll send you Marlee's contact details and you can ask her about it," Hettie said, opening her phone. "It might have turned up, but if she can't find it in the Battye collection then it simply can't be there. Sadly, items do go missing occasionally."

"Thanks for that," Belle said as her phone pinged with Marlee's contact details.

"I have to say, this murder doesn't feel like anything I've been involved in before," Hettie went on, reminding herself at the same time that she wasn't, really wasn't, actually investigating a murder. But it was difficult not to think of it as you tried to put the family information together.

"I feel like there aren't any real suspects," she went on. "There are possible family connections but no individual to point to who might have done it. Also, I didn't mention it before, but Gwen and Larry were down south at the weekend and were in Denmark on Sunday. Alicia's death was the talk of the town. She wasn't overly popular there either it seems. Someone even said Jackson's life might be more pleasant now his wife has gone."

"Wow. Her murder may be personal after all, and nothing to do with Lily."

"Could be." A chat with Jackson Feldhurst might be a good idea. She could hear Gwen's laughter ringing in her ears. Not investigating indeed.

Belle pulled up outside Hettie's house.

"Thanks for coming with me today."

"My pleasure. See you at the Club tomorrow night."

"Byee."

Hettie had hoped to visit her parents for afternoon tea today, but it was past that time already. She rang her mother and arranged to call in next morning. Her next task was to speak to Romola and run through the details for the Open Day before Thursday evening's committee meeting. And then there was that green folder waiting on her desk, but she knew she didn't have the energy to look through that. More family history was more than she could take today. But regardless of what she needed to do, a knock on her door found herself talking to Stuart Higgins instead.

Chapter 11

"**I**'m more involved in this murder investigation than I have been in the previous deaths here," Stuart explained, as they sat at Hettie's kitchen table with coffee and biscuits. Hettie wondered if that meant Grayson was pulling back from investigations in Woody Lake. She realised, with some surprise, that she was relieved at the thought of not bumping into him as often.

"Someone's realised that local input is helpful, have they?" she asked.

"They've always known that, Hettie," Stuart said, in a 'no comment' tone. "What we are interested in right now is the person who gave you the information about Roderick Johnson."

"Alicia Feldhurst's old boyfriend? Why do you need to know that?" Marlee wouldn't be pleased.

"Why can't you just tell me?" Stuart challenged, tilting his head as he looked at her.

"I can, it's just that I was asked not to if possible. Is it really necessary?"

"It is."

"Can you tell me why?" Stuart just raised his eyebrows at that. Hettie sighed. "It was Marlee Grainger, who you spoke to at the cemetery. Roddy Johnson and Alicia were part of her sister's group of school friends, who apparently continued to be friends into their early twenties. Sophie Grainger is five years older than Marlee. Or something around that, anyway."

"And how long have you known Marlee and Sophie?"

"I've never met Sophie. I only know what Marlee has told me about her in the past, which was very little, and now in relation to Alicia."

"You've told me you met Marlee at teacher training and then lost touch. What else can you tell me about her?"

"We lost touch because Marlee took a teaching position at Port Hedland when we graduated. I don't know how long she was there, but I didn't see or hear from her for almost twenty years. Then I met her again about four years ago when I was taking a Sixth-Grade class on a visit to the State Library, and she was there in the Battye. She'd left teaching and done some studies in librarianship and history."

"She was at the cemetery on Saturday doing research, is that correct?"

"Yes. Her application for a grant to fund her travel for further research has just been approved."

"Thanks for that information, Hettie."

"Is Roddy Johnson a suspect?"

Stuart gave her a wry grin. "Okay. The Johnson-Alston matter that came to the attention of the police some thirty years ago wasn't a clearcut case of him abusing and stalking her. There were allegations on both sides. The investigating officers suspected there was a third person involved, someone who was causing at least some of the trouble. Whether that was with the knowledge of either party, or acting on their own behalf, wasn't clear. In the end, a restraining order was issued for each complainant against the other."

"Has Roddy Johnson been in trouble since?" Hettie asked.

"Nothing that has come to the attention of the police. He has been questioned about this death, and his time is fully accounted for."

Marlee hadn't got that right then. She'd said Roddy had spent time in jail for abusing someone else. It wasn't the only thing.

"Marlee did say that one person wasn't happy about Alicia and Roddy's relationship back in the day," Hettie said. "Sophie was also interested in Roddy. It seemed to have broken her friendship with Alicia at the time, although they may have been in touch again in later years."

"That's Sophie Grainger?" Stuart confirmed.

"Yes, but I think she's married. I know Marlee has several nieces and nephews, but no idea what Sophie's married name might be."

Stuart was making a note on his phone. Marlee would know where the information came from if the police interviewed Sophie. If she was the suspected third person during Roddy and Alicia's trouble, could it have been Sophie whom Alicia fled south to escape, and not Roddy Johnson?

"I also need to ask if you had a chance to talk to the Feldhursts when you accompanied them to the cemetery on Sunday," Stuart was saying. "If they said anything in passing that might be helpful."

Hettie shrugged. "They were just struggling to make sense of what had happened. They didn't seem to have any idea of why someone would target Alicia anyway. We did wonder if Jackson had time to drive up from Denmark, kill his wife, and get back home that day without anyone being aware he was gone. You know," she added, as Stuart gave her a wry grin, "the spouse is always the first suspect."

"He was one of several possibilities, but he has a solid alibi for Friday, unless the two fellows he was working with have lied for him. All avenues are being investigated. Homicide was also looking at a road rage angle. There was evidence her car was involved in a tussle somewhere that day. Apparently, there was no damage to it when she left home early Friday, but there was evidence on the passenger side of contact with another vehicle."

"Oh, my. And it wasn't reported?"

"Not all minor collisions are, but the person who caused the minor damage to Alicia's SUV has been contacted. There was an angry exchange at the time of the incident, the anger being on Alicia's part, according to the other person involved. He gave her his phone number, and she immediately called it to make sure it was his phone that rang. He was annoyed at her for not trusting him, but he has an alibi for the rest of Friday and was nowhere near Woody Lake when she was killed."

"So, no murdering spouse, and no road rage."

"No. This case is presenting quite a challenge as it happens."

"She might have annoyed someone else who did follow her to the cemetery," Hettie suggested. "Although she didn't go straight there. According to Belle she booked into the Airbnb first." A road rage incident was as good an explanation for Alicia's death as anything else, Hettie supposed. It could certainly explain why it happened where it did.

"I suppose Belle told you that Keira Feldhurst asked her to go ahead and write the story her mother was researching?" Hettie said now.

"Did she?"

"You didn't know that?"

"I haven't spoken to Belle again." Hettie wondered if Grayson's team hadn't shared everything with Stuart. This could be awkward.

"The police do have a copy of Alicia's family research, though, don't they? I mean they've already spoken to the Baileys."

"The Baileys? Are we talking about Leighton Bailey here?"

"Well, yes, he's a member of the family. He's Cynthia Bailey's son. She was a Leadworth."

"Just a minute. Are you saying the Bailey's have a connection to Alicia Feldhurst's family research?"

Now Hettie was confused. "I thought the police must know all that. I'm sure it was Grayson I saw leaving the Bailey's place in the Valley this morning. And Leighton did complain about the police questioning them. Why else were they there?"

"Leighton Bailey was the person involved in the road incident with Alicia's car," Stuart said. "Does that clarify matters for you? I'd certainly like them clarified for me."

"No. Wow, that's some coincidence. If it was a coincidence."

"What do you know, Hettie? What have you been doing?"

"Okay. Well, as I said, Keira Feldhurst asked Belle to go on with writing up her mother's research and gave her a thumb drive with the information Alicia had for her. But there are still questions that Alicia needed answers to, so Belle and I spoke to Cynthia Bailey this morning in an effort to sort out whether Alicia's grandmother, Lily, was a Mason or a Leadworth. Cynthia's father grew up with Lily. Alicia had also wondered if Lily's daughter might have been fathered by a member of the Sandridge family. We had lunch at Valley Oasis and spoke to Kimberley Sandridge. According to her, Lily was pretty much part of the family for forty years or so, and they knew Alicia growing up."

Stuart was staring at her. "You've been going around interviewing possible suspects in this murder?"

"No, Stuart, of course not," Hettie hastened to say. "We talked to them about the family connection with Alicia's grandmother, based on Alicia's family research that Belle is working on for Keira Feldhurst." Hadn't she already said that? "Both Leighton Bailey and his mother told us they'd been interviewed by the police, so we figured you had Alicia's material."

"Hettie, even if we had it, if Alicia Feldhurst was asking questions and stirring up trouble that got her killed, what in heaven do you two think you were doing? Following in her footsteps? If these people are involved in some way you need to let the police deal with it."

"Well, we'd be happy too, Stuart. I can give you the thumb drive that Keira gave Belle. But we weren't asking about where all their family members were on the day Alicia died, for goodness' sake. All we did was try to clarify the information in Alicia's research."

"And did you?"

"Not really," Hettie had to admit. "There's a missing diary and a lot of conjecture." All they really had were more questions, and the vague idea that Alicia's murder could possibly, but only possibly, be linked to Lily's story. Somehow.

"I'll get that thumb drive for you," she said, and went to her study to fetch it. "It does surprise me that the police don't have this," she said on her return to the kitchen. "Shouldn't you be getting information from family members in a murder investigation?"

"Shouldn't family members be providing information to police?" Stuart countered.

"Perhaps the Feldhursts don't believe Alicia's death has anything to do with her family research."

"Which it may not have, of course, but we do need to follow up every lead, however tenuous. Have you spoken to Detective Fox about this?" Stuart asked now.

It was Hettie's turn to stare. "No, why would I do that?"

Stuart cleared his throat and looked down at his phone.

"Why did you go talk to Cynthia Bailey, anyway?" he asked. "I mean, you're not the one writing up this research, are you."

"Belle asked me to go with her." Hettie decided not to mention Belle's reason for asking. Safety in numbers would expose her to another telling off for getting involved with possible suspects.

Stuart leaned toward her across the table. "You'll be the death of me yet, Hettie Parke."

There was exasperation in his voice, but something else too. Drat Belle for putting ideas in her head. She did like him, and she'd always thought he was more than a bit attractive, which made her wonder if she really did have thing for men in uniform. Grayson had been a Sergeant too, when she was dating him. Hettie felt her face grow warm and she looked down at her coffee mug, now empty.

"Would you like another coffee?" she asked, to cover her confusion.

"I'll take a rain check on that, thanks Hettie," he said, picking up his cap from where he'd put it beside him on the table. "And thank you for the discussion and the thumb drive. We'll certainly be taking a look at it. But check with me first before visiting anyone else who may be involved, okay? I wouldn't want anything to happen to you."

Hettie said she would. She didn't fully register Stuart's last words until he was gone.

Next morning, Hettie sat on the sofa under the front window with her coffee and a biscuit, enjoying the sunshine that brightened and warmed the north-facing room. Outside she knew the air had the chill of mid-winter, mild as it was by many standards. The washing was in the dryer, the kitchen floor mopped. Her mind hadn't been inactive either. Everything she'd heard yesterday from Cynthia Bailey and Kimberley Sandridge, and what she'd re-read of Alicia Feldhurst's research, was rattling around in her brain trying to make connections.

Belle was going to check with Marlee about locating Poppy Mason's diary. She was glad she'd not called Marlee herself after what Stuart had told her yesterday. Cowardly, she knew, but she'd give it some time for the dust to settle before talking to her friend again.

One thing they hadn't thought about doing, which was so obvious it was almost embarrassing to think about it now, was to check with the person who'd written the essay. Kendall Philpott saw the diary in 2014 when she used it as the background for her essay. Surely there couldn't be too many people with that name in Australia. Hettie picked up her phone from the coffee table and googled it, hoping for a quick solution. The two hits that came up were for people in America. One was a minor female tennis player, and the other a male jazz musician in his sixties. Neither fit who she was looking for, and now she didn't even know if the Kendall Philpott she was looking for was male or female.

One step forward and two back, but if she could locate another student from that Post Grad course, they might tell her something about Kendall. She very much doubted that the University would provide contact details for anyone who'd been enrolled there. Privacy was becoming an increasing issue, rightly enough. Was there a chance she would recognise a name among the contributors? Or she could just google them all until she found one she could talk to.

If she went to the Murdoch University library and looked at the book itself, she could get the names of the students who had been in same class as Kendall from the list of contributors. Or, better still, she'd ring and ask if someone could photocopy the contents page and email it to her. That was much more sensible than driving an hour or more each way and trying to find a parking spot when she got there.

She opened her email app and discovered that Belle had sent her a copy of the cemetery photo Rhona had taken of Cynthia as a child. She'd enhanced it sufficiently for some of the faded wooden grave markers to be readable. Hettie could just make out the name 'Oliver Mason' on the wooden cross marking one small mound. The equally small mound right beside it was partly covered by a tree branch that had broken the wooden cross. It must have been the grave for Oliver's brother Charles. Marlee would be able to make use of the photo. She forwarded it to her email address with a brief explanation.

Her phone pinged with a reminder that her parents were expecting her for morning tea. She'd contact the Murdoch library later.

Chapter 12

"**W**e're in the Orangery, Hettie," Callie greeted her, when Hettie knocked on the door of their villa. "Isolde is here."

Hettie hoped Isolde Reflex's presence was social and not the result of a problem requiring the Parke Trust lawyer. She followed her mother to the back of the villa where the enclosed patio was now known as the Orangery, complete with lush greenery, and cane wickerwork furniture. She had to admire the quality of whatever her mother did even if she didn't always agree with the idea. Callie was wearing a floaty kaftan in black and purple today, a change from her neat, fitted outfits. Was this a new idea too?

"Don't get up, Dad," Hettie said going to her father before he could struggle to his feet. She bent and gave Jack a hug as he patted her shoulder. "Hello, Isolde," she said turning to the lawyer on the other side of the coffee table.

Unlike Callie, Isolde was her usual trim self in a muted-coloured skirt suit, this one a dark grey. Hettie was struck with how well it matched the woman's equally trim, short bob, worn tucked behind her ears.

Isolde returned her greeting with a crisp nod. "I believe you were at the old cemetery when that woman's body was found on Saturday," she said, as Hettie sat down beside her mother.

Callie's mouth formed a moue of displeasure.

"Yes," Hettie replied shortly, hoping to spare her mother any more on the subject. Jack, however, appeared just as interested as Isolde.

"How are the police doing, Hettie? Any ideas on what happened to her?"

Callie heaved a sigh of irritation as she filled Hettie's cup from the cafetiere.

"It happened on Trust property, Callie," Isolde said before Hettie could reply, holding out her own cup for a top up. "As I was saying, we may need to secure the cemetery if people are going to visit and cause trouble there." So not a new topic of discussion then, Hettie realised.

"What do you know about it, Hettie?" Jack asked again. She decided providing a brief account might also bring up added information and possible suspects. Jack had lived here all his life, like Cynthia Bailey, when Woody Lake had first been part of a cattle and sheep station, and then a dairy farm.

Hettie recounted what had transpired at the cemetery, then briefly mentioned the meetings she and Belle had with Cynthia Bailey and the Sandridges. She remembered to pass along Tina's hello to Jack and ended with an outline of the police investigation according to Stuart.

"Florrie knew Rhona Leadworth quite well at some time, didn't she," Callie said to Jack. "They had a falling out about something a few years before Rhona died."

"I was knee high to a grasshopper when Rhona died, Cal. All I know is what Mum said about it years later to Cynthia. It was something to do with the homestead, something about paint colours that Rhona didn't approve of."

"Well, she certainly wouldn't be happy with it now, then," Callie said with a laugh. "I didn't know Cynthia was still alive. How is she?"

"In a wheelchair and not much of her," Hettie replied. "Did either of you ever hear anything about Lily Mason?"

Callie shook her head.

"The only Masons I ever heard of were those boys and their mother who were buried in the cemetery," Jack said. "Was she Lily?"

"No. That was Poppy. She was Lily's mother."

"Well, that's all very interesting," Isolde said. "It reinforces what I was saying about securing the cemetery. It could be vandalised and no one would know about it until months later. Having it on the news just encourages sightseers."

Hettie remembered the police tape loose around the site and had to agree. It would be a shame if the area had to be fenced and locked off, but this was the time they lived in. Did people have more respect a hundred years ago?

"Raise it at the next Trust meeting," Jack told Isolde. "I'll support some sort of fencing for the place."

As Isolde made to leave, Hettie remembered why she'd come.

"I'm planning an Open Day at the Club in three and a half weeks' time," she said. "We'll have the official opening of the new courts, and I was hoping, Mum, that you could officiate. You know, declare the new courts open and all that. Would you? I'd really like you to do it."

Callie's face flushed with pleasure. "Oh, what a lovely idea, Hettie. Thank you. I'd be delighted."

Hettie could imagine the cogs turning as her mother considered what she would wear to such an event. She returned her mother's smile.

"I'll have to give a speech, won't I?" Callie said. "What should I say?"

"Anything you like," Hettie told her, glad her request had been well received. "Pop can help you with that, can't you? If Mum needs any help," she added judiciously, as her father winked.

"So what date is this happening," Callie asked, picking up her phone from the coffee table. Hettie told her and watched as her mother put it in her calendar.

"I'll give you more details closer to the time. There'll be posters put up, and a notice in the *Record*." She explained what else would be happening on the day.

"How exciting. You'll come, won't you?" Callie said to Isolde.

"Wouldn't miss it for the world," Isolde said. She gave Callie a kiss on the cheek. "I must go. I'll see myself out."

Hettie accepted Callie's invitation to join them for lunch and enjoyed a pleasant visit. She had just reached home again when her phone rang. She wasn't surprised to see it was Marlee calling.

"Hello," she answered.

"I asked you not to say anything Hettie," Marlee shouted. Hettie winced and moved the phone away from her ear. "The police have been around hassling Sophie. Her husband's furious, and they're both mad at me. What have I ever done to you?"

"You wanted me to tell the police about Roddy Johnson," Hettie said reasonably. "And I told you, if they asked I'd have to say who told me about it. And they insisted. I didn't have a choice."

"Of course you had a choice. Don't be so stupid. You could have told them anonymously, anyway."

"What? Now who's stupid? Why in heaven would I do that? Anyway, so could you. You didn't need to involve me. Why did you, anyway?"

"Not everyone likes interacting with the police, Hettie. Just because you seem to enjoy their company."

"Whoa. You can do your own dirty work from now on, Marlee. They haven't arrested you, have they?"

"Of course not, why would they do that?"

"And Sophie's not arrested?"

"No."

"Good. No harm done then." She clicked off the call and sat, simmering. It had been much more satisfying ending a call like that when you could slam the receiver down.

Marlee had been way over the top and completely unreasonable. She wondered if the police had accused Sophie of being involved in the trouble between Roddy and Alicia thirty years ago. That could have angered her husband, especially if he was around at the time. And if he suspected it was true. Sophie could have been annoyed at Marlee for saying she'd fancied Roddy back then too.

What a mess. There was a friendship gone bust. It was as bad as being a teenager again. She got up and paced. She needed a walk. Ceefer might enjoy one too. Ten minutes later she was on her way to the Cafe, the bag slung across her body packed with water and a snack.

She should have known it wouldn't be a simple in and out. The Mrs. B's were at their usual table, Ceefer sitting nearby, as usual.

"Hettie, have you solved this latest murder yet," Mrs. Bronson asked, before she'd barely closed the Cafe door behind her.

"I'm not involved," Hettie informed them, a little more snippily than usual. She tried again. "How are you? You're looking better today."

"I have an appointment for the hip operation," Mrs. Bronson replied, with a grimace. "In two weeks."

"I know the whole idea of that must be stressful, but you're doing the sensible thing in getting it done. You'll be up and about again in no time, I'm sure. I just popped in to see if Ceefer would like to go for a walk. How about it Ceef? We can go to the Waterway Park, and you can scare all the dogs." Ceefer snickered. "I knew you'd like that idea."

Hettie went to the Cafe laundry to collect his harness and leash, and after a quick word with Violet, they set off. She was feeling brighter by the time they reached the footbridge over the Cygnet River, but then as she looked at the water, flowing slowly, she couldn't help picturing a raft with four boys. Had it happened here? Not too far off probably, with almost direct access from the homestead. She pushed the image away and hurried on.

In the Waterway, they walked around the river offshoot, watching the ducks. As usual, any dogs in the park gave Ceefer a wide berth. Hettie got herself a macchiato from the coffee stand and gave Ceefer some water and a snack. Sitting on a park bench, enjoying her coffee, she tried to figure out what was bothering her, and realised they hadn't met up with anyone on their walk.

Had she been subconsciously hoping Ceefer would lead her to someone who would help solve Alicia Feldhurst's murder? It had been their mode of operandi on previous murders. What was different about this one?

"You really don't want to be involved with this investigation, do you?" she said to Ceefer.

"Mruff."

"I wish I knew why. Well, it's been a nice walk, but I guess we may as well go home." She tossed her take-away cup into a nearby bin and packed up Ceefer's water dish.

He didn't need to worry, anyway. She was just helping Belle with her research. But she did want to find that diary. Its whereabouts, and its contents, niggled.

They headed for home. Back on the footbridge there was a man standing, staring into the water. He looked familiar.

"Jackson?" Hettie said, as she got closer. He started and turned a worried face her way. "Are you okay?"

He stared for a moment as if pulled back to the present from someplace else.

"Hettie isn't it?" he said after a moment.

"Yes. Are you all right?" she asked again.

"No," he said, turning back to the water. Was she about to hear a confession?

"I'm sorry," she said. "Death always takes us by surprise."

"I don't know how I can keep going without her. She was a natural. She had a great eye for design. Plants just flourished under her hands."

"It's only natural that you'll miss her," she offered, realising she was sounding like an echo.

"Miss her?" Jackson said. "Yes, I will. I don't know if I'll be able to keep the business going by myself. I don't have her flair."

Hettie wasn't sure if this was simply Jackson's way of dealing with his personal loss, or if he really did only see Alicia as a business asset.

"Are you staying somewhere nearby?" she asked.

"What? No. The police have released her room at the Airbnb, and I've come by to collect her things. We're taking her home tomorrow. Well, the undertakers are taking her, of course. The funeral is set for Monday. I suppose I'll have to advertise for someone to take on her work."

"I suppose you will," Hettie said. "Well, take care of yourself."

She moved on. What an odd man. If that conversation had been designed to convince her he hadn't killed his wife, it had worked. She wondered what the police had made of him.

Chapter 13

"**M**erroow?" Ceefer called loudly as he and Hettie were passing Elly's house. A slightly gentler, but just as penetrating, 'miaow,' came from their own garden.

Hettie knew that voice. Aurora. Trouble in a white fur coat. Ceefer broke into a trot as they rounded the letterbox and made their way up the driveway. Janelle Rice stood up from the garden bench by the front door, Aurora in her arms. She was wearing an elegant kaftan in shades of green today instead of her usual floaty, layered style. She looked quite attractive. She might even have lost some weight.

"Hello," Hettie greeted her. "If you're planning to leave Aurora for a play date, I'm afraid Wednesday is not a suitable time. I have croquet this evening."

"I know that," Janelle replied huffily. Some things didn't change, anyway. "I need to talk to you."

"Oh, well, come in then. I'll put the kettle on."

Once inside and out of his harness, Ceefer chased after Aurora as she raced around the living room and over the furniture in their usual manner of greeting after not seeing one another for some time. Janelle snapped her fingers, and the cats immediately settled themselves on the sofa as if that had always been their intention.

"That was impressive," Hettie said. "You'll have to teach me that technique."

Not that she had much hope of doing it herself really. She'd never been able to get her fingers to make that snapping sound, no matter how hard she tried. It had been a losing competition with Larry when they were teenagers. Gwen could do it too, she'd discovered, which didn't help.

Janelle settled herself at the kitchen table and produced one of her herbal tea bags as Hettie switched the kettle on and put out two cups.

"How have you been?" Hettie asked, politeness taking over.

"I'm fine," Janelle replied, "but you need to keep out of this murder investigation."

Hettie turned to look at the woman. "I'm not in this murder investigation."

"You are involved, if not directly, then incidentally. You found the body. You've got all the information."

Hettie put a plate of Anzac biscuits on the table. "Well, that is partly true I suppose. I was one of the people involved in finding the body, yes, but if I had all the information, I would know who killed Alicia Feldhurst, wouldn't I?"

"There's danger ahead," Janelle said, raising her voice in the aggressive tone Hettie had heard before.

"Merroow?"

"You're upsetting Ceefer," Hettie said, using her teacher voice. Janelle wasn't the only one capable of making a point.

"He's already upset," Janelle told her, but she moderated her tone just the same. "He knows you shouldn't be involved in this. Matters are coming to a head."

Hettie poured water into their cups and put Janelle's tea in front of her. She sat with her own coffee.

"What matters are coming to a head?" she asked. "What do you know about this murder?"

"I'm talking about the trouble in the universe. All the signs indicate that it's escalating."

Hettie did her best not to roll her eyes. Not that Loki story again. Murder was an unpleasant thing to be dealing with in its own right. One didn't need to look to the universe to find reasons for trouble and uncertainty. Humans were quite capable of providing that themselves.

"Janelle, as I said, I'm not investigating. I can't not do something that I'm not doing. If that makes sense."

Janelle leaned forward, an earnest, if frustrated, look on her face.

"Hettie, you've talked to people, including the police. You need to not talk about it anymore. Not even think about it. There's still a chance to avoid the worst of it."

"Okay," Hettie said slowly, realising the woman was serious even if she herself didn't understand the why of it. "I'll concentrate on the Club Open Day. But what do I do if someone wants to speak to me about it?"

"Walk away. Change the subject. Just leave it alone. There's danger. It's real. Someone will get hurt."

After Janelle had left, Hettie needed something to take her mind off murder, and suspects, and trouble in the universe. She wandered around looking for anything that would help her achieve that. In her study she saw the green folder on her desk and snatched it up. She took it back to the kitchen and made herself a cup of coffee. She'd immerse herself in Garcia family history for an hour or so.

It was only the second time she had opened the folder and it had only been cursory glance the first time. There had been an envelope in there then, with the article about the Mason boys and the Leadworth letters that she had given to Marlee, and which were now part of this latest murder.

The rest of the contents were the same as she remembered. There was the 1943 marriage certificate of Callie's parents, Heather Hamilton and Eduardo Garcia. Beneath it were Callie's birth certificate, papers showing the Garcia family tree, and the expired passports for Heather and Callie. These last two were dated 1960. That was the year Heather and Callie returned to Australia after Eduardo died.

Hettie looked over the family tree. There were Eddie and Gloria, the youngest children of Callie's older stepbrother, Dominic, and the only ones to move to Australia from America. Heather's name appeared, and Callie's, linked to Eduardo, branching off beside his first wife, Ana Maria, and their four children.

Hettie frowned. The youngest of their children had been born in 1946, three years after Callie and shortly after the end of the war. That was also around the time Heather had travelled to America on one of the 'war bride' ships to join Eduardo.

Hettie quickly pulled out the last item in the folder, the long narrow envelope marked Last Will and Testament. Eduardo Garcia, the grandfather she had never met, had died in 1959. Hettie unfolded the document, written on thick paper, and quickly scanned it. Her Garcia grandfather had left everything to his wife, except for some bequests. But the name of his wife wasn't Heather May, it was Ana Maria.

What did it mean? Well, it was simple enough. Eduardo Garcia wasn't Heather's legal husband. According to his will, when he 'married' Heather in Australia he already had a wife and family in America, and he was still married to Anna Maria when he died. Hettie's mother Callie was illegitimate. Did she know this? Of course she must. She was sixteen when her father died.

What had her mother and grandmother's lives been like in America? Hettie couldn't begin to imagine the shock her grandmother must have experienced when she arrived, looking forward to a new life, only to find she wasn't legally married to her child's father. And how had his legal family taken the arrival of this woman and her child?

Hettie's mind was spinning. What was she to do now with this folder? She couldn't throw out family papers. And she certainly couldn't give them to Callie. Her mother would be mortified for Hettie to know the truth about her birth. It didn't matter to Hettie, but she knew it would matter very much to Callie.

Did Aunt Alice know? Did Jack? Or had that secret been left behind in America? She thought Eddie and Gloria must know. Hettie wished she didn't. She wished with all her heart she had never seen the green folder.

The sun was still above the horizon when Hettie walked to the Club with Ceefer that evening, Janelle had sown the seeds of unease in Hettie's mind, even if she didn't accept the theory of trouble in the universe. She'd pass on Janelle's warning to Belle when she saw her this evening too, just in case, though the only danger she could imagine was that Belle would laugh at her.

She entered the Cafe, planning to have a quick meal before croquet, and saw Aunt Alice and Eddie sharing a booth. Eddie waved her over.

"Are you joining us?" he asked.

"Am I invited?" Hettie parried.

"What do you think?" Eddie said to Aunt Alice.

"Oh, she may as well sit down, I suppose."

Hettie laughed. "You two are in a good mood." She helped Ceefer out of his harness, and Aunt Alice slid over to make room for her.

"We're planning a holiday," Eddie told her.

"Oooh. Somewhere exciting?" This was just what she needed to take her mind off murder and threats of danger.

"We're taking the Ghan from Adelaide to Darwin, stopping off along the way to visit Ayer's Rock."

"Train journeys are the best," Hettie said. "But it's called Uluru now Eddie."

"Uh, yeah, course it is. Anyway, then we're launching ourselves at Europe.'"

"The grand tour," Aunt Alice said, beaming at Eddie. "The Eiffel Tower, the Louvre, a gondola ride in Venice, biking in Amsterdam, a cruise through the glaciers in Norway…"

Hettie shivered, and it wasn't from the thought of icy glaciers, but the idea of travelling in the land of Norse mythology. How far did Janelle's warning extend?

"When are you planning on doing this?" she asked.

"Next winter, the European summer," Eddie told her. Hettie relaxed a little. They hadn't finished with this winter yet. Plenty of time for any trouble to be over and done with.

"Well, that sounds just wonderful, and I really envy you, but I must eat now, or I'll be late for croquet. Have you ordered?"

They hadn't. Hettie waved to Tess, and they were soon tucking into Violet's lamb and potato bake, between mouthfuls of which, Eddie and Aunt Alice told her more of their holiday plans. By the time Hettie left them with their dessert, still talking, she was halfway to Europe herself.

Out on Court Two, Judy and several others were having a practice hit. Romola sat on the patio nursing a coffee, and a bacon and cheese croissant. There was a folder beside her on the table.

"This is dinner," she told Hettie. "I spent the last two hours putting the finishing touches to a lady dragon costume for Lara's school concert dress rehearsal tomorrow."

"A lady dragon."

Romola giggled. "It's all in the face. Long lashes, sweet mouth, alluring side glances."

"I'm sure it will look great. Dare I ask if you've managed to do anything for the Open Day?"

"Dare you indeed." Romola rattled off a number of items from Hettie's list she'd attended to and pushed the folder toward her. "There's a timetable for the day's activities in there," she said, taking another mouthful of her croissant.

Hettie took out the printed sheet and glanced over it. "You are a wonder, Romola Asquith, you really are."

"Aw, shucks."

Hettie grinned. "I've got Mum primed to open the new courts, Elly is working on posters, and Violet has the food trucks and Cafe menu in hand." She must remember to check on the progress of the posters tomorrow, too. They needed to get to the printer on Friday.

"We'll be able to present it as an organised event at the Committee meeting tomorrow night," Romola said, wiping her fingers on a paper napkin, her croissant done. "Have you spoken to George?"

"Ah, no. I'd best go do that right now."

"You best had."

"Can I have this?" she asked waving the timetable.

"You best had," Romola repeated.

Hettie went inside, crossing the croquet room to the passage leading past the kitchen, offices, and bathrooms, and ending at the bowls clubroom. She could hear Larry's voice as she opened the door. And then George.

"No one's said anything about this to me," he was saying. He spied Hettie. "When was I going to hear about this Open Day?" he demanded, his face reddening. Hettie wondered for a moment if being president of the Bowls Club caused this transformation from easy-going and pleasant, to angry and loud. She wasn't the cause of it, surely.

"Right now, George," Hettie replied, stepping into the room. She cast a quick look at Larry, who shrugged. She supposed she couldn't really blame him. He wasn't to know she hadn't spoken to George yet, but now she was in damage control mode and the bowls club members in the room were looking on with interest.

"Can we go into your office?" she asked George. "We can go over our - um - our preliminary timetable and see what you can add in there."

George, still fuming, nodded and followed her back into the passage. Hettie let him open the Bowls Club office door for her. Ten minutes later, after explaining that the food trucks and Cafe goodies would be available for the Bowls Club, and George having decided they could hold a Sunday club tournament of their own with some fun games available to whoever wanted to join in, all was smooth sailing once more.

"And how are things at home with you, George?" Hettie asked. "Has Fiona gone off on her travels yet?"

"She's working right now," George replied. "Saving up for her trip next year. Summer in Europe is what she's planning."

"Oh, that's interesting. Aunt Alice and Eddie are planning on doing the same. Perhaps they could meet up with Fiona at some point. Would it be all right if they got in touch?"

"Yeah," George nodded eagerly, sounding relieved that someone might be able to check on his daughter's welfare while she was away. "Yeah, I'd like that. Thanks, Hettie."

"I'll let Aunt Alice know."

George went back to his members in a better mood than when he'd left them, and Hettie returned to the croquet room, relieved that something had gone well at last. Perhaps it was a turning point.

Chapter 14

Club Captain, Tom Eastbourne, was dishing out the counters that assigned the court and the ball for each player's game. It made it a lottery as to who you would be partnered with, and who you would play against and was part of the fun.

"Court Three, white," he told Hettie. The sun was down now, and the court lights lit up the place. She hesitated. Where was Belle? She still hadn't told her of Janelle's warning.

"Wakey, wakey, Hettie. We're on Court Three," Jo Isaacs said, giving her a poke in the ribs.

Hettie flinched. It hadn't been a gentle poke but that was Jo, annoying as ever.

"I was looking for Belle." Hettie found herself defending her tardiness.

"She's not here," Jo said, as they walked down the patio toward Court Three.

"Are you sure?" It wasn't like Belle to miss Wednesday night at the Club.

"Of course, I'm sure," Jo said, sounding disgruntled. "She promised to lend me that latest Alexander McCall Smith book that's out. My book club is reading it this month. Now I'll have to go to her house to get it."

How inconvenient of Belle to cause you so much trouble over a free book, Hettie thought. She had the feeling this was going to be an exceedingly long game. As they laboured their way through the first three hoops, she was beginning to wish something would happen to call her off the court. She would have traded that wish away for almost anything when it was answered.

"Hettie, Belle's in hospital," Judy called from Court Two, her phone in her hand. "She's been mugged."

"I'll see what I can find out," Judy said, abandoning Hettie and Romola in the Joondalup Hospital waiting room.

She and Romola sat. All the way in Judy's car, Janelle's warning had kept running through Hettie's head. Was this attack connected to Alicia Feldhurst's murder?

A man and woman in their fifties were the only other occupants of the waiting room. The woman was hunched over, her arms wrapped tightly around herself. Hettie thought she was half asleep. The man looked as if he already was, sitting back with his eyes closed.

The woman looked up. "Do you know Belle?" she asked. Hettie guessed their croquet outfits might be a big giveaway for that connection.

"We are. Do you know her?

"We're Belle's neighbours. Stibbins. Gail and Keith. We live in the other half of the duplex."

"Hettie, and Romola," Hettie introduced them.

"I found her," Keith said, his eyes still closed. "I was putting the bin out. I could've missed her if I'd done it earlier."

"He always ends up putting it out after dark," Gail said.

"Just as well," her husband replied.

"I just hope she'll be okay."

"Do you know what happened?" Romola asked. "Judy didn't know much from the phone call." Which was from Belle's mother, she had told them.

"She was lying on her front lawn. I tried to wake her, but she was out to it," Keith said.

"She might have fallen and hit her head on the paving," Gail put in, clearly hoping for an accident.

"Or it could have been a mugging," Keith said.

"Or she caught someone breaking in," his wife added.

"It was good of you to come to the hospital," Hettie told them, wondering if they always shared a conversation. "What time did you find her?"

"About an hour ago. She was in her croquet outfit." This from Gail.

"It must have happened on her way out," put in Keith.

"She can't have been there for long, then, at least," Romola said. The Stibbins nodded.

Judy came back, accompanied by Stuart Higgins.

"How is she?" everyone wanted to know.

"She's conscious, but a bit groggy," Judy said. "No major damage it would seem, but they'll keep her in for observation overnight, at least. Perhaps longer. She's been hit on the back of the head."

"Who would do that? Do we have to put in a security alarm?" Gail asked her husband. "I don't think I feel safe anymore."

"It wouldn't hurt," he said.

"Can we see her?" Hettie asked, turning to Judy.

It was Judy's turn to shake her head. "Her mother is with her. She needs rest and quiet right now. No stimulation."

The Stibbins decided it was time they left, and Stuart said he'd call in and get a formal statement from them next day.

"Lucky I recorded Lego Masters," Gail was saying as they walked out.

Shock did strange things to people, Hettie reflected. Finding something familiar and comforting was one way of dealing with it.

"Did you all come together?" Stuart asked now.

"We came in my car," Judy answered.

"I can give you a lift home then, Hettie. I need to talk to you."

Hettie wondered what he needed to talk to her about, but couldn't see any reason, polite or otherwise, for refusing. Romola nudged her as they all walked out to the hospital car park.

"Who's been a naughty girl, then?" she whispered. "I wonder if he'll put the siren on for you." Hettie groaned.

"**W**hat is so important to talk to me about that you would make me the subject to all sorts of innuendos?" Hettie said, as Stuart drove his police issue Skoda Superb wagon out of the car park and headed north-east, the semi-darkness in the car making her bolder.

"Have I done that?" Stuart asked, all innocence.

"You know you have, Stuart. You could have just called in after I got home if it was important." She was going to be accused of having a uniform fetish after this.

"But I've saved us both time and trouble this way, haven't I?"

"Time, anyway. How is the Feldhurst investigation getting on?" If Stuart had something to say to her, she would get what she could out of it too.

"What have you and Belle been doing that might have prompted this attack?" Stuart asked.

Hettie frowned. "You think this was more than just a random mugging?"

"I'm looking at all options."

Janelle's warning came back to her with an unpleasant thump. She swallowed. "Only what I've already told you," she said. "It's the police who've been stirring up trouble, in fact. I had an angry phone call from Marlee Grainger today, blaming me for giving you the Roddy Johnson information, and setting you onto her sister. Who is equally unimpressed, by the way. This is the thanks I get for passing on what I learn."

"I thought you said Marlee wanted the Roddy Johnson information passed on?"

"She did, but when are people reasonable when something backfires? She obviously knew what would happen if she told you herself, hence asking me to do it so Sophie wouldn't be drawn in. Or at the very least wouldn't blame her little sister if she was."

"That never works, of course."

"Tell her that. I'm not sure we'll be speaking to one another any time soon. Is Sophie a suspect?"

"Not at the moment. But this is what happens when civilians get involved in police matters."

"But I'm not involved," Hettie said, her voice rising. "At least not intentionally. This is all stuff coming at me from the side." She suddenly remembered her meeting with Jackson Feldhurst. "I did speak to Alicia's husband again earlier today," she admitted. "Accidentally."

Stuart concentrated on passing a slower vehicle before asking, with deceptive calm, "How did you manage that?"

"I took Ceefer for a walk in the Waterway and Jackson was standing on the footbridge when we were coming home." She repeated their conversation. "He seems overwhelmed at the thought of his business going under because Alicia isn't there with her particular talents."

"Yeah, strange bloke. His alibi stands and we can't find a motive anyway."

"It didn't sound like he had one. So, what do you think happened tonight with Belle?"

"She was attacked; that's not in dispute. Her bag is missing too, which means whoever did it has her car and house keys."

"But her car is still there?"

"It is."

"Have they burgled her house then?"

"I'll hopefully find that out tonight. Her mother gave me her own set of keys for Belle's house. After I drop you at home, I'll be checking on it."

"I could come with you. I might be able to see if anything is missing or out of place."

"You know the house well?"

"Well enough," Hettie said, crossing her fingers.

In truth, she'd only been to Belle's house a handful of times, and neither of those visits were all that recent. But her eyes would be better than those of someone who'd never been there before, wouldn't they? And she did know Belle better than Stuart did. At least she found herself hoping so, for some odd reason. Stuart didn't comment and Hettie wasn't certain if he agreed to her going with him or not.

"Have homicide been told of the attack on Belle?" she asked.

"I passed the information to the group that's investigating Alicia's death," he replied.

"Do they think there's a connection?"

Stuart heaved a sigh. "They'll look into it. Why it would be is another matter."

Hettie agreed. She spent the next ten minutes looking out at the semi-darkness, as they passed through the undeveloped area that separated Rosny and Woody Lake from the more populated of the Perth northern suburbs. A train passed by on the line running beside the road, heading for the city. Street and house lights began to show up and she realised they were now driving through some of the Rosny residential streets rather than heading for her own home.

Belle's house was in darkness apart from the front porch light, which was on. There were lights next door in the Stibbins duplex half, but the curtains and blinds were all drawn, except for the one that twitched as they pulled up. It didn't surprise Hettie that the Stibbins were feeling a little uneasy right now. Their peaceful, safe neighbourhood had proved to be not so much.

A police issue Kia Stinger was sitting quietly at the kerb. Two officers got out and Stuart joined them, after telling Hettie to wait in the locked car while they made sure the house was secure. Hettie watched as one of the officers went around to the back of the house and Stuart, with the other officer, approached the front door. Guns drawn, they entered the house amid warning cries of, "Police."

Two minutes later, Stuart came out and beckoned Hettie inside.

"See what you think," he said, handing her a pair of plastic gloves.

She wiggled her fingers, struggling to get the gloves on as the plastic stuck to her skin. Why did plastic gloves not have powder inside them anymore? Was it an environmental thing?

Eventually she was ready, and they made their way inside, wandering through the living room, dining room, and kitchen, but seeing nothing out of the ordinary. There were a few dishes in the sink – a bowl, cup, and cutlery – most likely from Belle's meal that evening. The house had two bedrooms, one of which, Hettie knew, was Belle's study. Her desk sat facing French doors that she'd had put in to access the patio with its many potted plants. Unlike Hettie, Belle was a keen gardener.

"It's too neat," Hettie said surveying Belle's desk. The only items on it were a folder with a notebook on top, and a cup of pens and pencils. Belle was normally well organised, but her desk didn't look like this when she was working on a project. There'd be loose papers, and photos. Even if they were in a tidy pile, they'd be there. "And where's her laptop?"

"She might have put it away in a safe place, rather than leave it here on the desk where it can be seen through the French doors," Stuart said. They checked the desk drawers, the filing cabinet, and the bookcase without success.

Stuart had his officers search the rest of the house and Belle's car, but there was no sign of the laptop or any other computer or storage device. Someone had made a clean sweep. Hettie was getting a bad feeling about this. Alicia's laptop and thumb drive had been missing too, according to her husband and daughter, either taken from her car or from the Airbnb where she was staying.

Was someone trying to gather up all Alicia's research? To do what? Destroy it? And how had they known Belle had a copy of it anyway? The Leadworths and Sandridges had known, of course. She mentioned it to Stuart as he drove her home.

"Promise me you'll leave this to the police now, Hettie," he said. "Please. Whoever is involved is dangerous and desperate."

Hettie promised she would. It was just that she couldn't really understand how destroying Alicia's research would help when a DNA test would provide the answers to Lily's history. She was sure a court could order a test if someone made a claim for paternity or inheritance. What were they missing?

Violet was already home when Stuart finally dropped her off.

"How are you? Is Belle going to be okay?" she asked, giving Hettie a hug.

"She's doing fine right now," Hettie told her. "Her mother was at the hospital with her. How was everyone at the Club?"

"Some people went home early."

Hettie didn't find that surprising. She suddenly felt very tired herself.

"Do you want a coffee?" Violet asked, a frown on her face.

"Cocoa might be a better idea," Hettie said. "Thanks, love." She pulled out a chair at the kitchen table and all but dropped onto it.

"Merroow?" Ceefer jumped up onto her lap and bumped his nose under her chin. She sat and stroked his back as she drank her cocoa. A little later, after Violet had gone to bed, Hettie went around the house as quietly as she could and made sure all the doors and windows were properly secured.

Chapter 15

Hettie was called in to take the Sixth-Grade class at Rosny Primary next morning. She saw Violet and Ceefer off to the Cafe and took herself off to school. When she walked into the staff room at morning recess Frank had a mug of coffee ready for her.

"How are you this morning?" he asked. "And how is Belle?"

"I'm okay, thanks," Hettie said accepting the coffee and grabbing an Anzac biscuit from the tin on the table. Just the right balance of fats and sugar. "Belle was doing okay when I went to the hospital last night. I didn't get to see her myself, but Judy checked on her. I didn't realise you knew her."

"I do. Lovely, bubbly red-haired lady who writes people's stories for them."

"Uh huh."

"Do the police know what happened?" he asked.

"Only that she was knocked unconscious and some items stolen from her house. Access using her own keys. Her neighbour found her when he put out his rubbish bin."

"This place used to be peaceful and safe until you started finding bodies," Frank said. "You realise that don't you?"

"I'm not responsible for the bodies, Frank," Hettie said, and turned away. Apparently, she wasn't the only one on edge after the attack on Belle. Hettie moved down the room.

"He's just been appointed principal at Port Hedland High, heaven help them," Wendy Lawrence was saying.

"He was there as a class teacher back in 2009, when I was there," a male teacher Hettie hadn't seen before, responded. "He's not a bad bloke."

"Charlie Philpott? Not a bad bloke?" Wendy scoffed. "Misogynistic little sod if you ask me. I feel sorry for any female teachers in that school. You wait. There'll be a deluge of applications for transfer before the end of the year."

Hettie thought her ears must be twitching. Philpott?

"Is he married?" she heard herself asking.

"Hettie, for goodness' sake, you don't want anything to do with him."

"Of course not, Wendy. Give me a break. But is he married? Or was he?"

"He was married to a teacher from the primary school back when I was in Port Hedland, but he's on his own up there now, so far as I know," the other teacher replied.

"I don't suppose you know his wife's name, by any chance," Hettie asked now.

"Philpott?"

Hettie rolled her eyes. "Her first name would be helpful."

"Can't say I remember."

"But you must have worked with her at the primary school."

"I've worked at half a dozen schools. I can't remember the names of everyone I've worked with. Besides, she was married."

"Of course, she was. Thanks, anyway." Hettie nodded and moved away.

She knew there must be some odd looks behind her, and Wendy would be wondering if she'd had anything to do with Charlie Philpott in the past, but she didn't care. She had a lead on Kendall Philpott, the author who had read Poppy Mason's diary and used it for her essay.

All she had to do was call Charlie and ask if he knew a Kendall Philpott, whether she was his ex-wife or another family member. The trouble was, someone else she knew had worked at Port Hedland too, but the connections forming in her mind didn't make sense.

"I'm sorry, Hettie. I didn't mean to upset you earlier," Frank said, joining her in the staff room at lunch time, with his coffee and toasted sandwich. Hettie wasn't feeling sociable and was sitting off by herself rather than joining most of the other teaching staff around the main table.

"I'm sorry, too," Hettie told him. "This attack on Belle has put a lot of us on edge."

"You want to talk about it?"

"No."

"Really? You don't want to use old Frank as a sounding board?"

"Not today."

"Do you want me to go away?"

"Can't we just sit without talking?"

Frank put his arm around her shoulder and gave it a squeeze. Hettie felt tears welling and concentrated on her bowl of chicken salad. One day she would have to tell Frank how much she appreciated him. Just not right now.

Hettie drove home at the end of the school day without having tried to contact Charlie

Philpott, and now it was too late to call the Port Hedland school. He would have finished work for the day as well. She knew she could search for him online in the telephone directory and get his home number or a mobile number.

She also knew she was avoiding having her fears confirmed but consoled herself with the thought that she would tell Stuart and let the police deal with it. Although what could she really tell them? She couldn't see a motive, and the whole idea seemed far-fetched. It's just that it did fit with a lot of what had happened in other ways.

She pulled into her driveway. As she got out of the car a white Pajero pulled up behind her. Marlee smiled and waved to her through the windscreen before climbing out.

"Hello. That was well timed," she said.

Hettie did her best to smile back, hugging her bag to her chest. How well timed?

"What brings you here today?" she asked.

"I was taking another look at the cemetery and thought I'd drop in before I went home."

"You weren't afraid of being there by yourself then?" Hettie asked, leaning back against her car.

"A case of getting back on the horse," Marlee said. "I'd never be able to research cemeteries if I let myself get spooked by what I might find there."

"That's true. How are you getting on with the arrangements for your trip north?"

"They're going okay. Listen, Hettie, I could do with a toilet stop before I head home. Would you mind?" Hettie did mind but how to refuse? "A coffee would be great too, catch up on old times. I take it you've been teaching today?" She eyed Hettie's comfortable, smart-casual outfit.

Hettie felt her shoulders relax. Marlee's request was perfectly reasonable. She'd been building a worst-case scenario where none existed.

"Sure. Sorry, I'm just a bit tired today."

"That's exactly why I gave up teaching," Marlee said as Hettie let them into the house. "I always felt exhausted."

"Powder room is just there on the left," Hettie said indicating further down the hall. "I'll put the kettle on."

"Fantastic. No sugar for me."

In the kitchen, Hettie set about filling the coffeemaker and putting out mugs. There were several two-day-old chocolate muffins in the fridge. Thirty seconds in the microwave would revive them. Marlee was taking her time. The mugs of coffee were on the table, and the muffins were ready and she hadn't returned. Hettie's earlier feeling of unease resurfaced.

She went quietly across the living room and glanced along the hall. The powder room door wasn't completely closed. Had Marlee been afraid it would make a noise and alert Hettie that she had left the room? Her study was the first room off the passage round the corner. She could hear someone in there before she'd even reached the room. Marlee was bent over her open laptop, her back to the door.

Hettie stepped back. Not a clever idea to confront someone if they'd already killed one woman and attacked another. Time to get out of here before she said or did something that alerted Marlee to what she suspected. She hurried to the kitchen and grabbed her bag. She'd call Stuart in a moment. She'd slip out the back door and into Aunt Alice's yard. That way Marlee wouldn't know where she'd gone. She had just stepped out when a hand landed on her shoulder.

"Where are you going?" Marlee asked from behind. Hettie shook her off and stepped away onto the patio. It seemed a waste of time to make excuses. The grim look on Marlee's face indicated they wouldn't be believed anyway.

"What is this about Marlee?" she asked. "Why are you trying to destroy Alicia's research?"

"Why can't people mind their own business?" she hissed. "What does it matter to anyone what I did back then? I was just trying to get through my Uni course."

"You were the Kendall Philpott who wrote that essay about the Mason boys and their mother, weren't you?"

"Kendall. I hated that name. Have you any idea what it's like to be called Kenny when you were at school, and told that your parents must have wanted a boy and how disappointed they must have been to get me? I've changed my name by deed poll now, but back then I had to register with it at Uni."

"But why?" Hettie asked. "What's in Alicia's research that matters to you?"

"I don't care about her research, or Lily Mason, or any of them. It was that essay. I didn't know it had been printed in that collection until Alicia started asking about the diary. Oh, God, that diary. She wouldn't let it go. And when I told her the truth, she laughed at me. She thought ruining my career, ruining my life, would be so funny. She said it would serve Sophie right if her sister was brought down. I asked her what she meant by that, but she wouldn't tell me."

"Apparently," Hettie said, "the police believe Sophie was behind the stalking and abuse allegations that Roddy and Alicia were laying against one another years back. Alicia must have discovered or at least suspected that Sophie was involved."

"Sophie was?" Understanding dawned on Marlee's face. "And I…oh my gosh."

Marlee would never have asked her to give Roddy's name to the police to try and throw attention elsewhere if she'd known of Sophie's involvement.

"So what happened with Alicia?" Hettie asked. "How did she die?"

"She wouldn't let it go. About the diary. I lost my temper and pushed her. She hit her head on one of the gravestones and started screaming she'd have me charged with assault. So I had to shut her up."

Why would Poppy Mason's diary present a problem for Marlee? She and Belle had believed the diary was the answer, but not in the way Hettie was beginning to think now. Her mind felt like a slot machine as the tumblers started to roll.

"When did you and Charlie Pilpott break up?" she asked.

"Why?"

"Was it around 2014? Was that the year you were doing your postgrad diploma for library studies? It must have been a tough time for you. Working full time, studying, dealing with a marriage falling apart."

"I don't need your sympathy."

"Oh, Marlee. Poppy Mason never wrote a diary, did she? Those entries came from you. They were about how you were feeling at the time."

Marlee stared at Hettie for a moment before sinking down in the doorway, her head in her hands.

"I had to write that final essay. That's all I needed to do. I'd have the diploma, and I could move up. I had the newspaper article about the boys drowning in the river. I found it when I was researching old cemeteries nearby. But I couldn't think what to do with it, and I had no other ideas and no energy. I was exhausted. And then one night I was journalling, trying to get my head together, and I had this brilliant idea of using what I'd written to create the diary of the boys' mother. I'd done my research, and I knew she'd died shortly after, so why not from a broken heart? It made for a great story."

"It did," Hettie said, thinking how easily this could have been avoided. "But you gave your fake diary a library archive entry. If you'd said it was in private hands it could have just disappeared, lost, stolen, thrown away."

"I wanted it to look genuine," Marlee told her, looking up. "Can't you understand that? I'd found a newspaper article and a diary that it was linked to. That's how good I was at what I did." Her head dropped once more. "I'll never be trusted again when this comes out. They'll take away my grant. I'll have to leave the library. I'll be a laughingstock. I'll have to take some dead-end job where no one knows me. Or cares."

She didn't seem to realise it wasn't a fake reference in an essay that would end her career. It was killing someone.

"Why did you go to the cemetery on Saturday?" Hettie asked.

"I wanted it to be done," Marlee said. "I wanted her car to be found, and for her to be listed as missing, and then I could get on with my life. I couldn't bear not knowing what was happening. And then I saw her fingers. I was so glad I'd checked. I was going to go back and fix it, if I had to break her arm to do it, but those stupid old women saw it on the video. Aaah, how unlucky can you be?

"First you brought me that newspaper article, and those letters," she went on. "Then Alicia, of all people in the world, starts asking about the diary. It was like I was haunted. And then that friend of yours called yesterday asking about the diary as well. I figured I may as well keep going. What did I have to lose now? All I had to do was destroy all mention of that diary reference and I could face it out."

Hettie pulled her phone from her bag. It was time to call Stuart.

"No," Marlee cried jumping to her feet and knocking the phone from Hettie's hand. "Things go missing from the collections all the time. I've cut the pages out of that book in the Uni library too. No one's going to find that essay again. It won't ever be connected to me."

"Marlee, Alicia had her research stored on the cloud. I'm sure Belle did too."

"Oh, they did, but it isn't there any longer. And you don't have it anymore either."

"But the police do."

Marlee screamed. "You're not telling this story to anyone Hettie Parke." A short, very sharp knife appeared in her hand.

Chapter 16

Marlee lunged at her. Hettie backed away, holding her bag as a shield. It was the bag she used for school, large and tough. Right now, though she wished it were bigger. Marlee slashed at it. Hettie fended her off. When Marlee tried to get at her sideways, Hettie twisted and dodged, keeping just out of reach. They were much the same height and build. Hettie just hoped she was the fitter of the two.

Marlee now turned her full attention on the bag, stabbing and slashing. Hettie heard it tear with another knife strike. It wasn't going to protect her forever. Another strike caught her hand. It stung. She could feel the blood trickling down her fingers. Defence wasn't going to stop this attack, especially if Marlee targeted her hands. She had to get proactive.

She started to inch her way around, circling back toward the door. If she could get inside, she might be able to lock Marlee out. Or grab something to fight with and make it out front where she could at least run. There'd be people out in the park or the street. She couldn't go through into Aunt Alice's yard, or Elly's, now. It would put them in danger. Marlee was desperate and not thinking clearly.

She was almost at the door. Marlee was getting frantic. She was all but throwing herself at Hettie as she slashed at the bag. In another moment the bag would be in pieces. It wasn't going to protect her much longer.

She reached behind, fumbling for the door handle. Marlee took Hettie's momentary lack of focus to charge, knocking her back against the wall. As she raised the knife to strike, Hettie bent one leg back and pushed off, launching herself, pushing the remains of her bag in Marlee's face as the knife flashed in front of her. Just as she felt herself losing momentum something swished past her from above. Then Marlee was on the ground screaming, a black ball of fur attached to her head.

Hettie grabbed up the knife that Marlee had dropped. The gate to Aunt Alice's backyard opened and Violet and Frank burst through, followed by a wide-eyed Aunt Alice. Hettie's legs gave way beneath her, and she sank to the patio.

Hettie sat on the sofa, legs propped up on an ottoman. The ambulance officers had bandaged her hand – again. It was the same hand she'd hurt before when dealing with a killer, although she hadn't been attacked that time. Marlee had been taken into custody and handed to Grayson's homicide group, to be charged initially with attacking Hettie. She'd contacted Romola to let her know she wouldn't be attending the club's committee meeting that evening but knew her vice-president and the rest of the committee members would deal with the business on hand.

Ceefer mewed and looked up at her from his spot, curled up beside her. She stroked his back with her bandaged hand. In her other hand was a glass of red wine. One glass was all she was going to have tonight. She was almost half asleep already.

"You've had a hard day, too, haven't you," she told Ceefer.

Violet had told her how Ceefer had yowled at the Cafe door and bolted when a customer came in. She'd run after him, concerned because he was heading home. There she met Frank who had just knocked on Aunt Alice's door. As Ceefer leapt from fence to rooftop, and disappeared round to the back, they had gone through Aunt Alice's house to her backyard to see what the fuss was about.

"How did he know?" Stuart asked, not for the first time.

"Cats are very intuitive, Sergeant," Aunt Alice said from the comfort of her armchair.

"Stuart, please, Mrs. Slater. I'm off duty."

"Just as long as you call me Aunt Alice, like everyone else in the family, Stuart." Hettie cast her a sharp look. "Cats aren't the only ones with intuition," she said to her niece.

"Mruuff." Ceefer murmured.

Larry cleared his throat. "Another beer, Stu?"

"Ah, don't mind if I do," Stuart said.

Frank winked at Hettie, who stared into her glass and wondered how things had gotten to this point without her really noticing it. Not that she objected. It felt surprisingly right.

"Dinner will be ready in five," Gwen said from the kitchen, where she was helping Violet. Elly was setting up the table in the dining room while Rafe entertained their daughters at the kitchen table with a set of domino tiles.

"How hard is it to put out fish and chips?" Larry wanted to know.

"This isn't any ordinary fish and chip dinner," his wife replied. "This is a celebratory meal. Another killer has been taken off the streets."

"Right," Dan said, coming into the living room at that moment, pocketing his phone. "Story's in. Headline for tomorrow's *Record* will be Cat on a Hot Tin Roof."

"Mreeew," Ceefer complained, as everyone groaned in agreement.

"It's not hot, and it's not tin, boy," Eddie told him. "What's happened to veracity in newspaper reporting?"

"It wasn't my idea," Dan said. "Besides, a little fun with headlines is acceptable, so long as the story is correct. You need to catch the reader's attention, otherwise they just pass over it."

"Dinner is served," Violet announced, ending the conversation as everyone descended on the dining table. Ceefer padded off to the kitchen to enjoy his own generous bowl of fish.

Half an hour later, as everyone was trying to finish off the last of the chips with Violet's homemade tartare sauce, there was a knock on the door.

Grave Double

"You're too late," Larry said, "the food's gone already." But he got up to answer the door anyway.

"Merroow." Ceefer ran after him, as they heard voices.

"Hettie?" Larry returned, accompanied by Janelle Rice and a large Maori man sporting a broad smile. Janelle was carrying Aurora in her cat basket, and the man had a cardboard box in his arms.

Hettie stood up from the table and approached them.

"This is Ari," Janelle introduced her friend, who nodded to Hettie. "We're leaving for New Zealand tonight," she said. "I need to leave Aurora with you."

"Oh, well… How long will you be away?"

"I won't be coming back."

"Merroooow." Ceefer flipped the catch on the cat basket, and in a flash he and Aurora had raced into the kitchen, claws clicking on the tiles, and back into the living room.

"Enough of that," Stuart said with a snap of his fingers. Both cats stopped in mid-flight and padded to the sofa where they demurely settled themselves as if they'd never behaved any other way.

189

"Way to go, Stu," Larry told him. "Will they start up again if I snap my fingers?"

"Don't you dare," Hettie said. Aurora giggled. Hettie wondered if she'd entered a parallel universe. "What about the troubles?" she asked Janelle quietly. After what had taken place these last few days she was feeling more amenable to that particular idea.

Janelle shrugged. "You have all you need." Glancing around the room, Hettie decided she probably did. "Besides, I think the worst is over. For the time being, anyway."

"Well, I'll be glad of that."

"We need to go, *e ipo*," Ari told Janelle. "We've a plane to catch," he said, as Larry took the box containing Aurora's belongings from him. With alohas and best wishes from both sides, Janelle and Ari left.

"Well, that was sweet and swift," Gwen said. Hettie looked at Aurora and wondered if you could buy a device that made a finger-snapping sound. Of course, there were always Larry or Gwen to do the honours. Or Stuart.

It was Sunday. Violet was still asleep, enjoying the one day she didn't need to be up early and off to the Cafe, but Hettie had a task to perform. She helped Ceefer into his harness and they set off for a walk along the riverside. She didn't want to meet up with anyone this morning, even Sandra Alberts and her dog Brutus.

"We're just going to visit someone Ceefer," she told him. They walked further along the park and then followed the path made by many feet down to the bend in Old Dairy Road. Turning back toward home, they reached Eddie and Frank's house.

Hettie knocked on their door, hoping it wasn't too early. It was Frank who answered her knock.

"Run out of coffee, have you?" he asked, holding the door wide for her to enter.

"Something like that," Hettie replied. "Is you dad about?"

"And there I was thinking it was my company you were looking for."

"You already know I'm only here for the coffee. And toast." She could smell toast fresh from the toaster.

"Ah, of course Well you'd better come and have some then. I'm not sure I could deal with a Hettie low on coffee."

"I'm not sure I can deal with either of you at this time of the morning," Eddie grumbled as he put slices of golden toast in the toast rack. A loaf of Abbot's Bakery Country Grains was open on the kitchen counter. It was Hettie's favourite.

"Sorry to burst in on you this early on a Sunday," Hettie said. "But I need some help with something." She unclipped Ceefer's leash and took off the bag that was slung across her shoulder. She hung it on a chair before sitting.

"Help yourself to toast," Eddie said, pushing the toast rack toward her as Frank put a plate and a knife in front of her. "There's strawberry jam and marmalade." He turned back to put more bread in the toaster.

"Thank you." As well as the sweet spreads for the toast, there was also peanut butter, crispy bacon, and cheese slices. Frank handed her a coffee.

"So what do you need help with Hettie?" Eddie asked when they were all sitting, sipping and eating.

Hettie reached into the bag hanging on her chair and placed the green folder on the table.

"This was found in a box in the Community Centre storeroom several months back. It was in the bottom of a box filled with shopping receipts that Grandma Florrie seems to have saved. This folder contains Callie's family history. Garcia family history."

Eddie's hands stilled for a moment in the process of buttering a slice of toast. He wiped his hands on a paper napkin and reached for the folder. Hettie waited as he checked over the contents.

"You see why I can't just give it to Callie," she said, when he opened the will. "She would be mortified if she knew that I knew about that. You did know about it yourself, didn't you?" She held her breath. Had she inadvertently revealed something about her mother that Eddie hadn't known?

"Yes, Hettie I did know."

Hettie relaxed. "What was their life like in America, Eddie? For my grandmother and my mother. It can't have been...comfortable."

"I was only eight years old when my grandfather died, you know. Heather and Callie flew back to Australia not long after. As a child I remember them being present on certain family occasions. It was only when I was older that I fully understood the relationships."

"So they were accepted as part of the Garcia family?"

"I guess they were. Or tolerated at least."

"Several of my aunts, dad's older sisters, asked after Callie when we were visiting earlier this year," Frank put in.

Eddie nodded. "They did."

"Mum has never talked about those years in America," Hettie said. "I could understand why when I saw that will."

"So what do you want us to do about this?" Eddie asked. He still had the will in his hand.

"I was hoping you might give the folder to Callie. Tell her something like, you found this folder among your stuff, something you'd forgotten you had. I don't want to keep it, and I don't want to throw it out, but, as I said, I can't give it to her myself."

"You could say it was among some family papers we brought back with us," Frank said to his father.

Eddie nodded thoughtfully. "Yeah, yeah, I could do that. Sure." He put the will back in its envelope and then back in the folder, which he closed.

"Thank you, Eddie. I really appreciate it. It's a weight off my mind." She was about to ask Eddie if her father knew the truth about Callie's parentage but decided it really wasn't important. Callie was a Garcia and it was Garcia family business. The Parkes didn't really feature.

"I wouldn't mind another coffee, Frank," Hettie said holding out her mug. "And I'm expecting you to try out a game of croquet at our Open Day."

"I'll drink to that," Eddie said holding out his own mug for a refill.

Epilogue

Hettie looked out onto the bowling green and smiled. Larry and Stuart were teaming up in a game against George and Sandra Alberts. Larry was coaching Stuart as he'd only had one lesson previous to this. He was taking the whole Parke family connection in good spirits and seemed to be enjoying himself, but he hadn't accepted the idea of wielding a mallet yet. Time would tell on that. Hettie found the idea of having him as her doubles partner on the croquet court exciting.

Stuart had at least agreed to join her in a game later today to try it out and she was sure she could get him hooked. She had asked Tom Eastbourne and Belle to join them in a doubles match. She couldn't wait to see how Stuart reacted to one of Tom's roquet shots. He made lawn bowls look like the genteel sport that it was.

Behind her, on the croquet courts, visitors were learning how to swing a croquet mallet, while in the clubroom, the television screen displayed a GC World Championship Tier 1 final featuring Egypt and New Zealand. Over it all the mingled smell of pizza and grilled burgers coming from the car park made her mouth water.

"How is he getting on?" Belle asked, appearing at Hettie's side.

"Not bad. He and Larry enjoy each other's company, which is great."

"Fitting nicely into the Parke family, is he? I did tell you."

"Oh, shut up." Belle laughed. "You are doing okay yourself, though, aren't you?" Hettie asked. Belle had spent two days in hospital following her attack.

"I'm fine, so stop worrying. It wasn't your fault," Belle told her. "It was my idea to call Marlee about the diary." Which wasn't entirely true as Hettie knew she'd provided the contact details. "Besides, if you'd done it, you'd have been the one in hospital and then you wouldn't have gone to school next day and heard about Charlie Philpott in Port Hedland. The police would still be searching for the killer."

"Possibly," Hettie said. "But Marlee suspected I must have had Alicia's stuff too, after I forwarded her that photo of Cynthia at the cemetery that you'd sent me."

"See, that was my fault. We can share the blame."

"You know as well as I do there was only one person to blame."

"It needn't have happened if people were nicer to one another," Belle said. "Alicia could have just let that business with the diary go."

"I suspect she saw it as a way to get back at Sophie for the trouble she'd caused all those years ago. If she did. That, and the fact she wasn't a very pleasant person anyway."

"I guess. It still comes down to the same thing though, doesn't it?"

Hettie couldn't disagree with that. If she needed any proof of people being nice to one another, it was here today. Her heart warmed to see all the Croquet Club and Bowls Club members present, mingling as one, with husbands, wives, partners, and children.

The magician Belle had suggested they hire was doing a good job keeping the children entertained at the far end of the croquet patio. Mrs. Bronson, recovering well from her hip operation, was in a wheelchair, attended by Mrs. Braxton, and a younger family member, a niece, Hettie seemed to remember. She'd even seen her sister, Pearl, trying her hand with a croquet mallet. And Frank had finally agreed to try it out too. Wonders would never cease.

"Have you finished Lily's story?" she asked Belle.

"I finished it a few days ago. Keira seems happy with it."

"What is she going to do with it, do you know?"

"Well, just between you and me," Belle told her, "the three families have taken DNA tests. After what happened, they decided it was best to settle the matter once and for all. Lily Mason was not a Leadworth, and her daughter Ruby was not a Sandridge, as it turns out. No hidden secrets anywhere. Keira is planning to do some research on Ancestry to see if she can find out more about Lily's parents, and their families. She's hoping to locate cousins and aunts and all the rest. I may end up writing some additions to the story."

"I'm glad it's being resolved happily."

"Belle," Romola called from the patio door. "You're needed."

Belle went off to take a group of visitors for a croquet game, and Hettie went to the Cafe to check if Violet needed any help there. Fortunately, all seemed under control. Ceefer and Aurora were both present and on their best behaviour. Hettie still didn't trust the little

Persian completely, but they were managing to get along. She could be a sweet thing when she wasn't causing trouble, and she did seem to be calming down. She gave them both some attention before heading outside again.

It was soon time for everyone to gather out on the croquet patio for the opening of the Croquet Club's new courts. People were called in from the courts and the greens, and the croquet patio was crowded. Some were watching proceedings from inside the Clubhouse, the doors open so they could hear what was being said.

Hettie stood behind her mother, with George Engles on one side of her, and Stuart on the other. Stuart grinned at her, his blue eyes twinkling. It made her heart leap. She smiled back.

She turned her attention to what was going on around her. Callie, microphone in hand was giving a gracious speech, saying how proud she was of the Parke Clubs, and how everyone should take advantage of what they had to offer, the enjoyment they brought to their members, the health benefits for people of all ages, etc., etc.

Cameras and phones flashed around them. Hettie knew this would be on the front page of the *Record* come Friday. She could see Dan was recording the speech on his phone. Callie would be in seventh heaven. Eventually her mother declared the new croquet courts open. Hettie waved both arms in the air.

At the boundary between the old and new courts, Len Travers and Sandra Alberts saw the signal and released a net. Dozens of brightly coloured helium balloons escaped into the sky. The patio resounded with cheering and clapping, as more phones and cameras flashed.

Hettie took a step forward as other family members gathered around.

"The balloons were a lovely touch, Hettie," Callie said, "but such a shame you didn't just have them in the yellow and green of the Club colours."

Hettie heard Pearl's sharp intake of breath behind her.

"Your speech was perfect, Mum," Hettie said, smiling at her mother and reaching out for a hug. "Thank you so much for doing that for me."

"Anytime, Hettie dear, anytime," Callie replied, as she hugged her daughter in return.

THE END

THANK YOU for reading the Woody Lake Mystery series. If you enjoyed your read, please take a moment to leave a rating or a review on Amazon or Goodreads. Just a few lines letting others know what you enjoyed about the book. Reviews help other readers find books they might also enjoy.

About the Author

Irene Sauman writes historical cozy mysteries. Under her pen name, Rennae Todd, she has written cozy mysteries in a present-day setting. Irene is a retired historian who grew up on a vineyard and orange orchard by the Murray River in New South Wales. She was an avid reader and started writing stories when she was nine years old (including some quite dreadful poetry).

Now living in Western Australia, she has three children and four grandchildren, and a sister who beta reads her books for plot holes and to see how quickly she can solve the mystery.

When not writing (or reading), Irene watches tennis, plays croquet, and has a reasonably green thumb, which means very little dies in her garden, unlike in her cozy mysteries.

Irene and Rennae share a website irenesaumanauthor.com where you can learn more about their books which are available in ebook and print, and from online libraries.

Follow us on BookBub for new releases

Irene's BookBub page

Rennae's BookBub page

Our Books

Murray Valley Mysteries
by Irene Sauman

This series of four cozy historical mysteries is set in the eighteen-seventies on the Murray River where Emma Haythorne's comfortable life at Wirramilla, her family's sheep station, is about to be turned upside down. There's a murder, and an old promise raises its ugly head. She might be able to solve the murder, but what she does to avoid the promise leaves her with a share in a riverboat and a business partner who doesn't approve of anything she does, especially getting involved in murder. Would she have fared better if she'd honoured the promise?

Find out starting with Book #1 *Saddled with Death*.

Victorian Country Town Mysteries
by Irene Sauman

Read on from the Murray Valley Mysteries and follow Emma's life into a new decade.

It's 1884. Emma is settling into a new life in the country town of Echuca, the main port on the Murray River. She is thankful to have Janey and Abe for help and company, but she's not sure what to do with herself.

But where Emma is concerned murder is never far away and once she gets involved with one, others follow. She soon has more than enough to fill her time as fellow residents prove interested in her herbal remedies, despite there being doctors in town, and there's also the Ladies Benevolent Society, providing they don't object to a member sullying her hands with suspicious deaths on occasion. Sergeant Donovan may one day even approve of her, though possibly not the coroner, Dr. MacArthur.

Join Emma in her new life. *Death in Disguise* is the first title in the series.

Miranda's Case Books
by Irene Sauman

Miranda Black, 62-year-old former British agent, is seeking a peaceful and uneventful retirement. Point Placid, a characterful seaside town on the west coast of Australia is just what she needs. Until she finds the body of the local historian on the beach, drawn to the scene by the cries of a black cat.

Amid the stories of smuggling past and present, a proposed development that has divided the town, and families who don't want their nefarious past brought to light Miranda can't help but become involved. After all she's used to getting things done outside of normal channels. And while the police aren't so keen on that approach Miranda's equally elderly neighbour and her out-spoken and bolshie niece are keen to assist and advise.

Can Miranda help solve a murder while still finding her place in her new hometown? Or will Point Placid be her undoing? This series is coming in 2026. Download the free series prequel here. Available in pdf.

Murray Valley Mysteries
Saddled with Death
A Gem of a Problem
A Body in the Woodpile
Murder at the Mill
Murray Valley Mysteries 1-4

Victorian Country Town Mysteries
Death in Disguise
Death of a Lady (2026)

Woody Lake Mysteries
Malice Aforecourt
Betwixt and Bewitched
A Christmas in July Sundowner Sally
Death by Candlelight
Grave Double
Woody Lake Mysteries 1-4

Miranda's Case Books
Murder at the Lighthouse (2026)
Murder in the Paint